THE FANTASY

Books by Thomas Hauser

Nonfiction:

Missing
The Trial Of Patrolman Thomas Shea
For Our Children (with Frank Macchiarola)
The Family Legal Companion
The Black Lights

Fiction:

Ashworth & Palmer
Agatha's Friends
The Beethoven Conspiracy
Hanneman's War
The Fantasy

THE
FANTASY

A NOVEL BY
Thomas Hauser

RICHARDSON & STEIRMAN
NEW YORK
1986

I.S.B.N. 0-931933-29-3

L.C.C. #86-82396

Designed by Neuwirth & Associates

THE FANTASY is published by
Richardson & Steirman, Inc.
246 Fifth Avenue
New York, N.Y. 10001

For Bruce and Priscilla

PART ONE

1

MY PARENTS MET at a college mixer in 1942. The Japanese had just bombed Pearl Harbor, and speculation was rife that, within weeks, the entire senior class at Columbia would be drafted. Still, college socials continued, and, one night in January, my father went to a mixer with his friend Albert Tenzer to check out the girls from Barnard.

The room, legend has it, was smoky and dimly lit. A five-man combo was playing Tommy Dorsey music while a hundred-or-so students milled about in dance, conversation, and awkward solitude. Albert was ready to write the evening off and go down to the Gold Rail for a beer when my father spotted two women talking animatedly in a corner.

"What about them?"

"Not bad," Albert admitted. "Tell you what. I'll take the blonde. You can have the brunette."

"Nuts to you. I get the blonde. I saw them first."

Slowly, like a man reluctant to take an unnecessary risk, Albert reached into his pocket. "Here's a nickel. We'll flip."

My father called tails. It came up heads.

Six months later, my father and the brunette were married.

That story is part of my heritage; and it reaffirms my belief in the interaction of fate and luck. A college mixer, a chance encounter, turning a corner and meeting someone on the street without any way of knowing how fully that person will impact upon your life . . .

I met Laura one afternoon when Big Walter and I were walking in the park.

For about a decade, Big Walter has been my best friend. He stands 6'3" and weighs 270 pounds. A lot of that is muscle; about 50 pounds is flab. Any doctor worth his salt would tell Big Walter to lose weight, but I've never seen a 270-pounder who jogs faster. Incidentally, it's always Big Walter—not Walter. His parents, his friends, his wife Patricia—everyone incorporates the adjective.

Five minutes with Big Walter will convince the bitterest of misanthropes to have faith. He's a prince and the Rock of Gibraltar rolled into one. Big Walter is a supportive loving husband and a trustworthy loyal friend. He's generous, totally without malice, and always cries at the end of *Snow White*. His problem is that, for the past eight years, he's been writing screenplays and, at age thirty-four, he doesn't have a dime to show for it. Not that his stuff is bad—it isn't. It's better than most movies currently on the market. All eight of Big Walter's action scripts (which include two westerns, two police dramas, three Nazi spy thrillers, and a hunt for buried treasure) are do-able. The same holds true for his love story and two comedies. But for every thousand screenplays written today, one gets turned into a movie, and Big Walter is without contacts. Ergo, for the past eight years, he's labored as superintendent in the building on West 78th Street in Manhattan where he and Patricia live. The job pays $100 a week plus free rent on their tiny one-bedroom apartment. Patricia, who ranks as the most understanding spouse this side of Jupiter, is the primary breadwinner. Not an ideal arrangement perhaps, but it gives Big Walter time to write, and I want you to understand something: he busts his ass. Big Walter works harder at writing than most people ever work, and that's not easy when screenplays keep coming back in the mail, getting crammed down your throat.

Anyway, that's Big Walter. And I suppose I should introduce myself. My name is Tom Hammond. Like Big Walter, I'm 6'3", but weigh considerably less. I grew up in Westchester, followed my father to Columbia, and graduated with a double major in English and government. Then I went up to Harvard for a Ph.D. in political science and, at age twenty-eight, returned to Columbia to teach. I liked teaching, but, after five years, the pieces didn't fit. Too often, I found myself sitting at my desk, preparing a lecture, being bored. More and more, I wanted to create—not just pass along or reinterpret what others did. Besides, there were times when I felt uncomfortably like an overgrown student. In sum, I'd had it with academia. Two months after my thirty-third birthday, I decided to leave Columbia to write. Now, to celebrate my first day of freedom as a free-lance writer, Big Walter and I had decided to check out the zoo in Central Park.

It was a perfect May day; temperature in the mid-seventies; the sky a brilliant blue. The park was close to empty, Monday being a workday for most New Yorkers. "If we had three hundred sixty days a year like this, I wouldn't complain about the other five," Big Walter noted.

Leisurely, we made our way past Tavern on the Green toward the South Lawn. "Did you hear about James Michener?" Big Walter queried. "He just got a three-million-dollar advance on his new book."

"With an income like that, I guess he can afford mushrooms on his pizza."

"With an income like that, he can afford a pizza with truffles on it! I think Michener and Robert Ludlum are saving up to buy the federal government." The next few minutes were spent contemplating the odds that somebody someday would give Big Walter $3,000,000. "No better than fifty-fifty," he posited.

Whereupon the conversation turned to other matters—professional and personal—culminating in a subject of perennial discussion: the absence of a girlfriend in my life. "I don't understand it," Big Walter lamented. "You're intelligent; you're good-looking; at times, you're nice. You're monogamously oriented, and we'll assume, for the moment, that you're good in bed. Isn't there some way you could trade in all your women for a wife?"

"Believe me, if the right woman came along, I'd grab her."

We walked in silence as Big Walter digested the comment. "You know what I think?" he said at last. "I think your standards are too high. You're looking for a perfect woman—a wife in shining armor—and in the process, you're writing off a lot of relationships that could have flourished. What about Janet?"

"She wasn't very intelligent."

"Carol?"

"Too self-centered."

"Sherry?"

"She went back to her old boyfriend last week."

Off to the right, an attractive dark-haired woman was on a course that would converge with ours twenty yards ahead.

"My standards are fine," I added defensively. "All I want is someone who's warm, loving, sensitive, sexy, and smart."

"How about her?" Big Walter asked, pointing to the right.

"Be serious."

"I am being serious. How old would you say she is?"

"I don't know. Somewhere between twenty-eight and thirty."

"Do you see a wedding ring?"

"No."

"And she's gorgeous."

"I wouldn't say gorgeous."

"Yes she is—confess it!"

Supercasually, I took a look. The object of Big Walter's attention was wearing well-fitting slacks and a blue plaid shirt. Her dark hair fell in waves, framing a face which in profile was flawless. It was the face of a woman who had been good-looking from birth and would continue to be beautiful whatever lay in the years ahead.

"Look at the way she walks," Big Walter prodded. "A woman with purpose; straightforward strides, directly ahead. And she looks nice."

In truth, she looked very nice. Also, at this point, I was starting to notice her figure, which was very good if not spectacular.

"Okay! She's very attractive. What do you suggest I do next?"

"Simple."

The paths converged.

With an air of solemnity, Big Walter cleared his throat and addressed the woman who was about to enter my life: "Hello! My name is Walter Walker. I'm of no interest to you because I'm married and woefully overweight. However, this is my friend, Tom Hammond, and he wants to meet you. Would you like to go to the zoo with us?''

That, in a nutshell, is how I met Laura Kinney—born in Waterbury, Connecticut, thirty years old, a "producer-slash-editor" for NBC News.

"Anyway, that's my title," she explained as we made our way through the park. "National News is coordinated in three eight-hour shifts. If a story breaks while I'm on duty, I get yelled at if NBC doesn't cover it."

"Why you?"

Laura shrugged. "I give out the assignments—not to Tom Brokaw or Roger Mudd; I don't mean that. But if there's news in Libya at three in the morning, someone has to make sure there's a camera crew and correspondent on location to pick it up. I'm on the midnight-to-eight A.M. shift. There are very few experiences in life that compare with transmitting videotape from Tripoli to New York at three in the morning."

In due course, we reached the zoo. Big Walter bought a box of Cracker Jacks and began tossing his booty piece-by-piece to a baby elephant. Most of the animals seemed old and sluggish. Laura and I exchanged further biographical data. She—Wellesley College, Columbia School of Journalism, a regular at Lincoln Center and the Metropolitan Museum of Art. Me—five years teaching, an avid reader, interested in politics and sports.

"You'll have to excuse me," Big Walter announced as the conversation progressed. "I'm about to return to the unenviable task of repairing the building boiler. Patricia thinks that being married to the superintendent gives her an inalienable right to hot water."

Munching on the last of his Cracker Jacks, Big Walter disappeared into the park. Laura and I spent the next twenty minutes by the seals, then left and began walking north. She was taller than I'd realized—5'7", maybe even another inch. Her stride matched mine.

"What made you leave teaching?"

"Boredom," I said, flattening my voice to emphasize the point.

"It must have taken a lot of courage to leave Columbia."

"Not really. For a while, I was intimidated by the prospect. But then I realized that I was the only person holding me back. I've always wanted to write. I grew up in a house where books were treated as something special. Finally I realized that my reservations about leaving Columbia boiled down to two factors: being afraid of not earning a living as a writer, and wanting to cling to an academic setting where there was always someone to share lunch. I guess I'm still scared that writing will be lonely; but, if it doesn't work, I can go back to academia. Technically, I'm on sabbatical for two semesters, and my savings will last a year after that."

"You're being modest. It's not that easy to shake up a comfortable life."

I liked her. I had from the moment we'd met. Things between us seemed to be falling into place.

"What are you planning to write?"

"A novel."

"Do you have an agent?"

"I'm not sure I want one. I've heard agents are nothing more than a maildrop for manuscripts."

A knowing smile crossed her lips. "That might be true, but most publishers won't read manuscripts from unagented authors. Sooner or later, you'll need help." Just for a moment, she paused, seeming to ponder a potential commitment. "I know an agent. His name is Augustus Hasson. Let me think about it."

At 72nd Street, we left the park. Past the Majestic Apartments, where my grandparents once lived; past the Dakota, where John Lennon had been murdered. Brushing a strand of hair from her cheek, Laura glanced at her watch. It was 2:00.

"Would you like to stop for a cup of coffee?" I asked.

"I don't drink coffee."

"How about a Coke?"

"I don't like Coke."

She was playing, waiting for whatever else I chose to suggest.

"Okay. At the risk of sounding forward, I made some wonderful fudge last night. Would you like to come over for a piece of fudge?"

"All right."

Dodging occasional roller-skaters and baby carriages, we walked the last few blocks to my apartment, a once-elegant prewar structure on West End Avenue.

"How long have you lived here?" Laura asked on the elevator going up.

"It'll be five years next month."

The elevator stopped and we disembarked. At the door to my apartment, I reached for my keys and let her in. Thirty plants of varying shapes and sizes were visible from the foyer.

"Very nice," she complimented. "How many rooms?"

"Three and a half. I'll show you around if you'd like."

We started in the foyer; then to the living room, where Laura stopped to examine titles on the wall-to-wall bookshelf. In the bedroom, again she homed in on the books. "It's a nice collection," she said, surveying the contemporary fiction and classics.

Last on the tour was a foil-covered pan on the kitchen counter.

"This is the famous fudge," I announced. "Would you like a piece?"

"That's why I'm here, isn't it?"

Taking a knife, I cut two three-inch squares and passed one to my guest. Laura finished her piece and cut half of another before returning with me to the living room and settling on the sofa.

"I admire what you're doing," she said, looking again toward the books. "There's a magical quality to good literature. But I think you'll find it frustrating as hell to write."

"What makes you say that?"

"I don't know. I guess it's the nature of the beast. Writers and artists are almost never satisfied with what they create. On Picasso's eightieth birthday, a friend went to visit and found him incredibly depressed. When he asked why, Picasso told him, 'It took me eighty years to reach this stage of artistic development. I've wasted almost my entire life.' " For the second time in as many hours, a rueful smile crossed her lips. "We all think we have so much time, and we don't. Each year goes by more quickly than the last."

I was starting to focus on her face. Lips that were red without benefit of makeup, sparkling teeth, brown eyes, a touch of color in her cheeks. In truth, it was difficult to take my eyes off her, and, not wanting it to show, I averted my gaze just enough to suspend eye contact.

"We're old before we know it," Laura said, continuing the thought. "Even children. My niece just turned four, and she's growing like a weed. Before anyone knows it, she'll be in college."

Thoughts kept piling up inside me as she spoke. This was a woman I had met two hours before in the park. We were strangers. It was New York. She should be wary. Just being in my apartment was taking a risk. And then, suddenly, I realized that Laura Kinney was in total control of the situation. And, far from being scared, she was orchestrating it exactly the way she wanted.

Laura leaned forward.

"Kiss me," she said.

Soon after.

The afternoon sun filtered in as we stood by the edge of my bed. Laura was wearing black panties and a lace bra. The lines of her figure were trim and taut.

"You have a nice body."

"So do you," she answered.

Just for a moment, I stepped back to run my eyes across her, and a vulnerable look—the first she'd shown—crept into her face. The moment passed and, moving closer, I touched her cheek. Slowly, she reached back to unhook her bra, then lowered herself to the bed.

"I suppose you think this is very strange," she said, drawing me down beside her.

"Actually, I think it's kind of wonderful—far and away the best thing that's ever happened to me in Central Park."

Again there was silence, followed by an awkward look on her part.

"Tom, do you talk when you make love?"

"Sometimes."

"So do I." Her eyes brightened.

"I can't stand it when someone says, 'Don't talk; we're making love.' You'd think they were playing bridge."

An hour later, we were wonderfully tired, emotionally exhausted, spent. The late-afternoon sun seemed softer than before, its flat rays reflecting off nooks and crannies around the room as we lay together. Laura's head pressed tight against the curve of my chest. A gentle breeze played at the edge of the half-open window. It all seemed very right. And then I realized that something had been welling up inside me all afternoon, from the moment we'd met—that, as strange as the whole thing was, maybe I had found someone who would change my life; that with time and encouragement, I could fall in love with Laura Kinney.

"You're very special," I whispered, touching a finger to her lips.

There was no answer.

Laura looked silently toward the ceiling, focusing on nothing.

"What are you thinking?"

Still there was no answer.

Then, finally: "Tom, there's something I should tell you. . . . I'm married."

2

LAURA LEFT AT 6:00. An hour later, after dressing and remaking the bed, I went over to Big Walter's for dinner. "He's still in the basement," Patricia announced, leading me inside the apartment. "Sometimes I think he has a thing going with the boiler."

Their living room was small and sparsely furnished with leftovers from other people's apartments. No two pieces of furniture matched, but the collection managed to achieve a certain charm and warmth. Patricia—slender, dark-haired, and quite pretty—sat on the sofa beneath a yellowing page set in a crude dime-store frame. Torn years before from an obscure literary journal, it beckoned to be read:

*   *   *

KANSAS SUNSET
By Walter Walker

Each locale has its own special way
*   Of ushering in the night*
The way of the plains is soft and warm
Deep greens and blues
Settle over the land
*   Till*
By virtue of its silent conquest
Darkness is King

The poem was Big Walter's first. Together with a teen love story conceived in a moment of financial desperation and sold for $90, it comprised the sum total of his published works. Hanging nearby, an eight-by-ten photo of the Acropolis commemorated the Walkers' honeymoon in Greece.

"What's new at the office?" I asked, settling in a chair opposite Patricia.

"Not much. The boss is going to Italy for some wholesale buying next month. That's about it."

"Any word on your raise?"

"Not yet. Given the way he operates, he'll put it off as long as possible." Inside the kitchen, a timer sounded. "Keep me company while I baste," Patricia suggested, rising to administer to a half-cooked brisket of beef. "I want to hear all about the woman my husband reports picking up for you this afternoon in the park."

Big Walter returned from the basement at 8:00, victorious and covered with soot. "The boiler's fixed," he announced, disappearing into the bathroom to wash up. Soon after, he emerged, examining his forearm through a tear in the elbow of his green-and-white horizontally striped shirt.

"How did things go in the park?" he asked, sinking onto the sofa beside Patricia. "When last I noticed, you were on the verge of making a date."

"Not exactly."

"You didn't blow it, did you?—not after my phenomenally charming and irresistible introduction."

"Not exactly," I repeated.

"Then, please—what happened?"

Step by step, I recounted the day's events. Our walk through the park, Laura's aversion to coffee and fondness for fudge, the tour of my apartment, her request for a kiss.

"Then what happened?" Big Walter pressed.

"I kissed her."

"And?"

"It was a good kiss."

"What about after that?"

"I kissed her again."

"Then what?"

"We went to bed."

A moment of silence was followed by a look of immense satisfaction on Big Walter's face. "Well, I guess that proves what I've always said. Never make love in the morning if there's a chance you'll meet someone more interesting after lunch."

"You approve, then?" I prodded.

"Absolutely. A true lady never makes love by conventional appointment."

His joy at having engineered my encounter with Laura was overwhelming.

"Big Walter," Patricia cooed sweetly. "There's something else Tom should tell you."

"What?"

"Laura Kinney is married."

*   *   *

Dinner was excellent. It always was when Patricia cooked.

"I'm not quite sure what happens next," I admitted, helping myself to a portion of broccoli as I recounted the day's events. "After we made love, Laura said she had to leave, and that was it. Tonight, she works from midnight till eight; then she goes home to sleep. She promised she'd call sometime tomorrow."

"Do you want to know what I think?" Big Walter asked.

"No."

"I'll tell you anyway."

"Your advice I don't need. You're the one who introduced us—remember?"

"All right. Then you tell me: what's next?"

"I don't know. I've slept with a lot of women in my life, but never one who was married."

"Under the circumstances, I'd say you're not culpable."

"Maybe not for today. But if Laura's willing . . . Everything happened so fast, I didn't have time to think. Which reminds me——" Reaching back, I took a ball-point pen and creased sheet of lined yellow paper from my pocket. "This afternoon, when we were making love, I thought of a plot twist for the novel. Let me write it down before I forget."

"I don't believe it!" moaned Patricia. "You're as bad as Big Walter. He gets his biggest erections in midafternoon when he sits down to write." Ever so briefly, she paused for effect. "For someone who weighs two hundred seventy pounds, it's amazing how little he is."

The expected wail of protest was immediately forthcoming: "Patricia!"

"Yes?"

"How can you say that?"

Dramatically, she rose from her chair, threw her arms around Big Walter, and gave him a kiss. "The fact that we're married and I love you means I can say anything I want."

Dinner continued, with the conversation touching on a wide range of subjects. Meanwhile, the food kept coming, and Big Walter ate everything but the design on his plate. "I'm in favor of the New York State bottle law," he held forth at one juncture, when the discussion turned to environmental issues. "But you have to admit: life was simpler without it. I mean, paying thirty cents extra every time you buy a six-pack of beer or soda and then lugging empty bottles back to the supermarket for a refund might be ecologically sound, but it's a pain in the neck."

"It would be much easier if you didn't keep forgetting the law and throwing empty bottles in the garbage," Patricia countered.

"She's amazing," Big Walter noted, turning in my direction. "You won't believe this but, after every meal, Patricia counts up empty bottles the way rich people check their sterling silver. I can't tell you how many times I've had to pick through the garbage looking for an empty Budweiser bottle like it was a twenty-dollar fork."

About 11:00, I left and went home to sleep. Drifting off, I mused on the fact that, eight hours earlier, I'd been lying beneath the same covers with a woman I hadn't even known when the day started. I liked Laura. I liked her a lot. But I wasn't sure what to expect next, or even whether Laura would call, as promised. For obvious reasons, she hadn't given me her home telephone number. If I had to, I supposed I could track her down at work, but common sense suggested she wouldn't like that. I hoped she'd call; she had promised.

The following morning, with Laura still on my mind, I got up, shaved, showered, and began day two of my career as a free-lance writer. The basic plot for my book had been long in the making. My hero was a CIA operative named David Barrett, who would join forces with an absolutely stunning oceanologist named Carolyn Hewitt. Together they would pursue a lode of energy-producing crystals that had been discovered somewhere on the South Pacific Ocean floor. For almost a year, I'd jotted down miscellaneous thoughts, character traits, and anything else that seemed relevant to the envisioned novel.

Overall, my methodology was fairly efficient. Whenever an idea came to mind, I'd write it down on an available piece of paper. Then, usually at night, I'd transfer the day's thoughts to 4″ × 6″ index cards. Over time, the pile of cards had grown to well over a thousand, stacked neatly in a steel-grey file box on the bedroom shelf. A few more weeks of research and organization, and I'd be ready to write. Before that happened, though, it seemed eminently sensible that I read some books with an eye toward what was selling and how to write it.

I'd started with John LeCarré and Robert Ludlum, then Frederick Forsyth and Ken Follett. Finally, I'd come to Graham Greene, enjoying him most because his characters had a depth that few contemporary writers matched. Now, waiting for Laura's telephone call, I studied *The Human Factor*—the only Graham Greene novel I hadn't read.

"Combine GG-type character development with greater action," I noted on a sheet of lined yellow paper. "If you can," I added, marking an asterisk next to the second comment. At noon I broke for lunch, then went back to work, finishing *The Human Factor* around 3:00. Killing time, I transferred the notes I'd taken onto index cards at my desk:

Make David Barrett a driven character, heroic but haunted by his past. It's essential that the reader find him sympathetic.

Plot twist: Consider making Carolyn Hewitt a double agent, but not if it hurts the love story.

Laura called at 5:00. There was the mandatory "How are you?" and "How was your day?" Then—"I'd like to see you," she said.

There's a black marble fountain on the plaza at Lincoln Center, where we agreed to meet. Somewhat anxiously, I passed a few minutes watering my plants before walking to Broadway and 64th Street, where Laura stood waiting by the fountain's edge. I waved. She walked toward me. "Let's have a drink," she suggested, pointing to an awning-covered café midway between the fountain and Avery Fisher Hall.

We commandeered seats and a young waitress took our order. Laura was dressed very much like the day before: casual clothes, a simple but elegant gold watch. A tiny diamond hung from a gold chain around her neck. Again I realized how much I liked her—and how little we knew about each other. For a moment, we made small talk. The waitress brought our drinks.

Then Laura came to the point: "I want to apologize for yesterday afternoon. Whether or not going to bed with you was right, I should have told you beforehand that I was married."

I waited. After a moment, she went on. "My husband Allen and I met nine years ago—just after I graduated from college. That's about the time a person starts to realize there's more to life than United States foreign policy and whether your parents will let you have the car on Saturday night. Early on in our relationship, we dated other people. Then, for a while, we stopped seeing each other. We got back together; things grew more serious. Six years ago, we were married. I was twenty-four. He was thirty. In case you're wondering, we don't have any children.

"I suppose on some levels I'm very lucky. Allen is loyal, reasonably sensitive, generous, and very smart. He loves me as much as he's capable of loving. We have a nice life-style and, all things considered, for most of the marriage, our sex life was pretty good. All the trimmings are right. I remember joking when I moved in that his kitchen even had counter space for me to cook.'' An emotional cloud touched her face. ''What I'm trying to say, what makes it so difficult is, Allen isn't a bastard. In some ways, I love him. But I don't respect him. I don't want to be married to him anymore.''

I sat there, listening, pushing whatever guilt or identification I had with anonymous Allen to the back of my mind. Two Chagall murals shone through the giant plate-glass windows of the Metropolitan Opera House. Holding on to her composure, Laura continued.

''I guess, from the beginning, I knew it was wrong. I remember, about a week before we got married, telling myself 'I really don't love this man the way I ought to. There has to be something more.' But instead of being honest, I pushed my reservations aside. I took my doubts and I blocked them. This was a man I loved, or at least I was attracted to him. He was brimming with qualities I admired. And, besides, the commitment had been made. The wedding was set. So I convinced myself that I was suffering from normal premarital jitters and that everything would turn out all right.''

''And?''

''The wedding was fine. It was like a big party, and I'm great at parties. The honeymoon was fine, too, except Allen kept reading the International Edition of the *Herald Tribune* and, after a while, it started to bug me. Then we settled down as young newlyweds, and I told myself, 'Well, things aren't perfect, but the package is pretty good.' I was back in school by then, and I decided to take life one day at a time. Study hard, get involved with a good book, see a movie with a friend. It wasn't bad. I fantasized a lot, I flirted, but up until yesterday, I was always faithful. And there were times when the marriage worked.

"About a year ago, Allen decided we were ready to have children. And I said no. I want children someday; I really do. But his asking forced me to face the fact that the marriage might end. In a sense, it shocked me. I'd never dealt head-on with the possibility of divorce. And then it shocked me again when I realized that for five years, we'd never communicated with each other about what was wrong with the marriage. Since then, it's been all downhill. Allen has been trying desperately to hold on. One minute, he smothers me with need. The next, he's angry and bitter. Meanwhile, my fantasies have grown and become more and more important. About a week ago, I found myself imagining that this basically decent man I've been married to for six years was dead. That's when I realized that no wizard's wand or witch's spell will turn my life around. I have to do it myself. For six years, on one level or another, I've wanted out. Last week, I decided to do something about it."

The café was becoming more crowded as couples began arriving for a light dinner before the New York Philharmonic's evening performance. Two middle-aged men took seats at the next table. Laura lowered her voice just a bit.

"Since last week, things have happened pretty quickly. Saturday I took my ring off. Sunday I started sleeping in the spare bedroom. Monday I met you."

"What made you come to my apartment?"

"I don't know. Testing the waters, I guess."

"Is that all?"

Pressing her lips, Laura leaned forward just a bit. "Tom, I like you. I like what you're trying to do with your life. But the truth is, I was ready for an affair. It didn't happen by accident. Timing was ninety percent of it." A self-conscious smile crossed her face. "I don't know why I'm telling you all this. I guess I feel I owe you an explanation. And I need someone to talk to. I'm scared stiff.''

The waitress came by to see if either of us wanted another drink. Then there was silence between Laura and myself—an indication that it was my turn to speak.

"How does Allen feel about all this?"

"Confused, angry, disoriented, hurt. At first, he tried jokes: 'Getting married is like going into a restaurant. You order what you want. And then, when you see what the other fellow has, you wish you'd ordered that instead.' That's how Allen handled the matter a year ago. Then he opted for long discussions: 'Be honest, Laura. Give me all the *facts*. If I have the *facts*, we can work it out.' After that, it was hostility. That lasted about a month. Now despair seems to be in vogue, coupled with burgeoning depression.''

Lifting her glass, she took a sip. "Allen never really supported me emotionally. I don't think he knows how. There's a blind spot on his emotional retina, but he's an expert when it comes to inducing guilt. Somehow, he's made me feel as if I'm responsible for his life, and I can tell you without qualification that you're talking with a woman who sees a lot of pain and suffering ahead.'' Again, the smile— rueful and self-mocking. "Life hasn't turned out the way I thought it would.''

"Don't blame yourself. If getting your act together was easy, everyone would do it.''

"Thanks! You're sweet.''

"Really, I'm just as confused as you are. If I had all the answers, I'd be married now with two-point-three kids.''

Outside the café, the line of people waiting for tables was growing. The couple next to us left. Laura looked down at her watch. "I've got to go,'' she said, reaching for the check.

"Let me treat.''

"No way. I owe you for the fudge." Signaling for the waitress, she placed a ten-dollar bill on the table between us. "Tom, thank you. You've been very nice."

Another couple advanced toward our table. The waitress brought Laura's change and we left, moving past the fountain, to the street.

"Can I walk you somewhere?"

"No, thanks," she answered. "I have to go home and do a few things before work."

I wanted to hold on. What to say next?

"I'd like to see you again," I said a little tentatively. "Would it be all right if I called you at work?"

"I rather you didn't."

"Does that mean I won't see you again?"

There was a pause that lasted for what seemed an eternity. "All right," Laura said at last. "Sometime next week, I'll call you for lunch."

"Is that a promise?"

Again the pause.

"Yes, Tom. I promise. . . . But there's something I want to tell you, and I mean it. You and I aren't going to get involved with one another—ever."

3

WEDNESDAY MORNING, I went up to Columbia to do some research for my book. The campus was largely deserted; most students had gone home when exams ended. Outside Furnald Hall, I stopped to chat with an assistant dean, then walked on, skirting the well-manicured shrubs and lawn, past the sundial where angry students had rallied in Vietnam War days, to Butler Library—an immense six-story building with Ionic columns beneath a facade that bore the names "Homer. Plato. Aristotle. Demosthenes. Cicero. Virgil." Briefly, I wondered if someday the university trustees might add "Hammond" to the inscription. Then I figured that Shakespeare and Dickens hadn't made it, so I probably wouldn't either.

Inside the library, I flashed my faculty ID card to the guard on duty, who nodded and waved me on. Then I climbed the stairs to the third-floor reference room, where rows of file drawers cataloged Columbia's 7,000,000 volumes. I began with the topical subject index, spending several hours noting call numbers for close to thirty books. After that, I broke for lunch at a nearby deli, came back, and journeyed to level six in the stacks, where the first few volumes on my list were located.

"I know you," the checkout librarian announced as I emerged with my find. "You're Professor Hammond. I took your course in American Politics last autumn."

"Was it any good?"

"For sure, yes! But how come I only got a C-plus?"

In due course, I extricated myself from the conversation and settled at a long oak table in the reading room, opposite an elderly man who was poring over a heavy economics text. Pen in hand, I began to read, jotting notes on my index cards as I went. By 5:00 P.M., I'd read through three books and accumulated a stack of index cards an inch high. Satisfied, I went home for dinner, watched a movie on television, and returned the next day for more. Every so often, sitting in the library, I'd lean back and daydream, running my eyes along the endless rows of shelves. Mostly, though, I focused on the task at hand, and the next few days passed quickly as my outline took shape. Over the weekend, I went jogging twice, saw a play, and, Sunday night, had dinner with Big Walter and Patricia. This time, it was my turn to cook, so I invited them over for filet of sole amandine and salad.

"The Caesar salad is very good," Big Walter complimented as we ate. "But it would have been better if you'd washed the sand out of the lettuce before you made it."

"Some people would be polite enough not to notice."

"Not really," he countered. "Polite enough not to mention it, maybe. But anyone would notice."

After dinner, we settled in the living room and traded literary gossip: an underground rumor that Walter Cronkite was negotiating to write his memoirs with Barbara Tuchman; Arbor House had reportedly offered Sidney Sheldon a four-book contract worth $10,000,000; Oriana Fallaci was (or was not) planning a book on the Ayatollah Khomeini.

"I understand that Norman Mailer wants to market his own brand of wine," Big Walter said. "He figures Paul Newman did it with salad dressing, and wine shouldn't be any different."

Every now and then, Big Walter will make an outrageous statement just to ascertain whether you're listening or not.

"I read about it in a wine journal I get each month," he persisted.

"Big Walter, when did you start getting wine journals?"

"Long ago. Back in college, I was a connoisseur. Then I stopped drinking the stuff because it didn't agree with my stomach."

Somehow, I had the feeling I was being set up.

"I'll prove it," he continued, pursuing the point. "Put a blindfold on me, and pour a glass of wine without telling me what kind it is. Two sips and I'll identify it."

"You're kidding!"

"No, I'm not. Two sips and I'll be able to tell you what kind of wine it is."

"Big Walter, I'm calling your bluff."

Patricia went into the bathroom for a towel that we tied around Big Walter's eyes. Then I went to the closet, where several bottles of wine were stashed, and pulled out a nondescript-looking bottle of burgundy labeled "Chateau Lamet."

"Big Walter, you're about to be put to the ultimate test."

"No problem. I promise, you'll be impressed."

Corkscrew in hand, I opened the burgundy and poured several inches into a long-stemmed glass. "Here you are, sir," I announced, handing the wine to Big Walter.

Patricia looked on with a certain knowing confidence.

Majestically, Big Walter lifted the glass to his nose for an exaggerated sniff, then lowered it to his lips and took a sip. He rolled the burgundy around his tongue before swallowing, then took another sip.

"All right," I pressed, "what kind of wine is it?"

The glow of victory lit up his face.

"Red," he said.

On Monday morning, I returned to the library to continue researching my book. Because the plot centered on energy-producing crystals discovered on the ocean floor, it was important for me to get the scientific facts straight. Deep-sea mining was treasure hunting on a scale that boggled the imagination. Three-quarters of the earth's surface lies under water, and within that murky realm there's enough mineral wealth to alter the world's balance of power radically. Enough copper to last for 6,000 years, compared to 40 years' known reserves on land; enough nickel for 150,000 years, as against 90 by surface mining. Still, no one knew precisely what lay on the ocean floor. The surface of the moon is better charted than the sea. Earlier in the year, a team of scientists had photographed an object believed to be a rock on the ocean bottom. Three months after their study began, the "rock" got up and moved a foot-and-a-half. Then it sprouted an arm and grew. The temperature at deep-sea depths was 35°. No light whatsoever filtered down. It was a world of pitch-black chasms deeper than the Grand Canyon, chains of peaks that rivaled the Himalayas, flat plains that stretched for miles on end. One by one, as I read on, my index cards mounted:

Fifty percent of the earth's surface lies two miles or more under water.

Multinational consortiums and government-backed enterprises are developing the technology to bring deep-sea minerals to the surface. In a matter of years, deep-sea mining at depths of 15,000 feet will be a reality.

Tuesday, I turned to the *Reader's Guide to Periodical Literature* for additional sources. By Wednesday afternoon, my research on deep-sea mining was complete. Satisfied with my progress, I closed up my attaché case, took the subway home, and telephoned Big Walter to see whether he wanted to go jogging.

"I'd love to," he said. "Give me twenty minutes to finish some odds and ends, and I'll meet you on the promenade in Riverside Park."

That arranged, I changed into running clothes and walked over to the promenade. Big Walter wasn't in sight, so I began alone, jogging north to 90th Street. Then I turned, and, on the way back, spotted a familiar figure lumbering along.

"Let's pick up the pace," Big Walter ordered. "I'm trying to break eight minutes for the first mile."

We ran along a path overlooking the Hudson River. The pace was a little slower than I'd have done on my own, but still comfortable. Like most joggers, I run because I enjoy it, and one of the reasons I enjoy it is the camaraderie with Big Walter.

"I have an idea for a new screenplay," he announced as we passed 80th Street. "Patricia likes it, and I'm curious to know what you think."

"Shoot."

"It's about the Pope and his illegitimate son."

"You're being redundant. If he's the Pope, his son couldn't very well be legitimate."

"I know. Anyway, let me tell you the plot. As a young

priest living in Italy, the Pope-to-be visited the United States and fathered an illegitimate child. Now, years later, the child has become an American priest. And the Pope, unaware of the link between them, has elevated his son through the church hierarchy to the College of Cardinals. Then, at a Vatican convocation, the two come face to face. There's an extraordinary facial resemblance, and they start to compare notes on their past. Meanwhile, a cardinal who's jealous of the son's growing reputation and power is starting to catch on. There's a hundred different ways I could end it.''

''Not bad,'' I admitted. ''But chances are that no studio will be willing to produce it until the Catholic church becomes extinct.''

''I guess that's right,'' Big Walter conceded, a forlorn look clouding over his face. ''But what if——''

''Hold on a second,'' I interrupted. ''There's something I want to write.''

''What?''

''I want to take a note. That man over there—the one in the wheelchair feeding pigeons. He must be eighty years old, but he's still giving out sustenance and life. I can use that someday in a book.''

''But we're in the middle of jogging.''

''Go on ahead. I'll catch up.''

''You're nuts.''

''No, I'm not,'' I said defensively, still matching his stride.

''Yes, you are. You're absolutely bonkers.''

Despite his protestations, Big Walter stopped while I made my note with the pen I always carried. Then we went on, past the playground, along a row of benches where an elderly husband and wife sat holding hands together.

''I was thinking this afternoon about the creative-writing teacher I had in college,'' Big Walter noted, embarking upon a typical stream of consciousness. ''The first day of class, he handed us each a sheet of paper and told us to write a detailed physical description of ourselves. Then he took the ones written by the good-looking women home and jacked off reading them that night.''

"How do you know he jacked off?''

"Believe me! I know. I could see it in his eyes while we were writing the assignment.''

The trail led down a hill to the water's edge, then up an incline to where we had begun on the promenade overlooking the river. Suddenly, Big Walter's pace slackened. "Why don't we stop for a minute?'' he suggested. "You can write another note.''

"What's the matter? I thought you were out to break the eight-minute mile.''

"I was, but suddenly I don't feel so good. I think it's the three jelly donuts I ate right before jogging.''

Patricia was working late that night, so, after Big Walter and I washed up, we went out alone for dinner. The place was a neighborhood dive that served Cuban food with heavy emphasis on rice, refried beans, and garlic. Most of the cooking was done by the restaurant's owner, a heavy, dark-haired woman named Juanita Imbalzhno, and it was pretty good. Also, at $4 per complete dinner, it was a bargain. Thus it was that a goodly number of Imbalzhno's patrons lived in fear that the restaurant would someday be "discovered" by *New York Magazine,* which undoubtedly would lead to a deluge of trend-seeking customers and, of course, raised prices.

"Just think,'' Big Walter noted as we settled at a formica-topped table. "Someday literary historians will look back on our dinners here with the same reverence as Round Table sessions at the Algonquin.''

"Maybe, but I wouldn't count on it.''

The waitress came and threw some silverware in front of us. After appropriate deliberation, I ordered arroz con pollo; Big Walter, shredded beef with a side order of plantains. The other patrons were mostly Hispanic. The tables were close together, but somehow conversations didn't seem to intrude on one another. For a while, we talked about how the New York Yankees were doing, then classical music, and The Great American Novel (our chosen designation for my work in progress). Toward the end of the meal, Big Walter asked how I'd feel if he licked his plate. "Be honest," he prodded. "Don't you ever lick the plate when you're alone at home?"

"Yes."

"Why should a restaurant be any different?"

"Big Walter, you're impossible."

"No, I'm not. Difficult, yes, but not impossible."

Eventually, the conversation turned serious, as it often did when Big Walter set aside his protective good humor. We talked at considerable length about the frustrations inherent in his not being able to earn a living as a writer, and whether I'd face the same problem in the years ahead. Then, inevitably, it seemed, the conversation turned to Laura.

"She's on your mind, isn't she?" Big Walter asked.

"I guess so. It's been eight days since I heard from her."

"Maybe that's good. After all, she is married."

"Believe me, I'm very much aware of the fact, and it's not something I take lightly. I keep telling myself not to think about her, but that kind of self-control has never been my strong point."

"What do you plan on doing?"

"I don't know. I suppose I could put on a suit, go over to NBC with a dozen roses, and tell her I thought we had a date for dinner tonight. But somehow I don't think it would work. And besides, getting more involved will probably mean getting hurt, so I guess the best thing to do is concentrate on my work. Incidentally, I meant to ask you something. The day Laura and I met in the park, she mentioned knowing a literary agent named Augustus Hasson. If she does call, is there any point in asking her to—— Hey! Are you all right?''

Before my eyes, Big Walter was turning a very excited shade of red.

''What's the matter?''

''Tom, you've got to be kidding!''

With surprising speed, the red in Big Walter's face was working its way toward purple.

''Kidding about what?''

''Jesus Christ! Tom, haven't you ever heard of Augustus Hasson!''

4

A WORD ABOUT literary agents—not because I like them, but because they're the grease that enables authors to slide into the publishing process.

Once a book has been written, the author faces an essential question: "How do I get it published?" The answer, I was to learn through a tortuous process of trial and error, lies with a literary agent.

Basically, agents offer four services: (1) They can get a publisher to read a manuscript (and, given the number of unsolicited works that rain down upon publishing houses, this in itself is an accomplishment). (2) An experienced agent knows which editor at which publishing house is most likely to be receptive to a particular book, and will direct his client to that editor for safekeeping. (3) A good agent is able to build a publisher's enthusiasm for a given project and lend credibility to an unknown writer; and (4) An agent with good business sense knows how to negotiate a contract that protects his client's interests.

In return for these services, most agents charge ten percent off the top of the writer's earnings. To many, this fee seems exorbitant. After all, most authors spend thousands of hours writing a book. It doesn't take an agent hundreds of hours to sell it. Also, an unfortunately high percentage of agents are incompetent. They don't know one editor from another and have next to no business savvy. Thus, good agents are at a premium, and the average writer in search of one comes face-to-face with a rather brutal Catch-22. Good agents won't take him on because the writer isn't an established money-maker. Meanwhile, a bad agent might, of necessity, lend a hand; but bad agents don't sell books. The result is that most writers (like Big Walter) wind up with incompetent agents who send out manuscripts, get back a pile of rejection slips, do nothing for several months, and then instruct the client to find another agent. It was after a particularly dismal encounter with one such soul that Big Walter opined, "Agents are parasites. They belong in the ninth ring of Dante's Inferno with landlords and muggers. But," he added quickly, "I'd love to have a good one."

Within the literary community, a handful of agents have risen to prominence. Owen Laster, Sterling Lord, Mort Janklow, Julian Bach. Add to that list Lynn Nesbit, Candida Donadio, a half-dozen others, and you have a group as exclusive as any collection of Fortune 500 corporate executives. These agents make books happen: *Princess Daisy,* a paperback sale of $3,200,000; *Fools Die,* $2,550,000; *Whirlwind,* $5,000,000. The tab, of course, is picked up by the buying public: *Valley of the Dolls,* 16,000,000 copies; *Shogun,* 7,000,000; *Iacocca,* 2,600,000 copies sold in *hardcover* alone.

In sum, getting a good agent is quite a coup. And good

agents, in turn, are always anxious to acquire a blockbuster author. By and large, the biggest authors are scattered one-to-a-customer: Norman Mailer with Scott Meredith, Robert Ludlum with Henry Morrison, John Irving with Peter Matson, and so on. One blockbuster author makes an agent happy. Two will make him rich. *Augustus Hasson had a dozen.* And, among publishing's inner circle, his rise to prominence was legendary.

Hasson was born in New York to parents of modest means on the eve of the Great Depression. As a young man, he dabbled at writing, attended Harvard on scholarship, and, at age twenty-two, went to work for the *Saturday Evening Post* as an assistant editor. For three years, he cleaned up after errant writers, correcting their syntax and soothing egos. Then Marcus Salinger, the premier literary agent of his day, took a liking to Hasson and suggested that he give agenting a try.

Hasson went to work for Salinger at age twenty-five, and, for two years, was a model disciple. Unlike many of his contemporaries, he worked incredibly long hours, often reading authors' manuscripts until 3:00 or 4:00 A.M. He had a rare gift for picking out what would sell and quickly learned the nuances of squeezing every last dollar from an editor when blessed with a property the editor wanted. Salinger, who was nearing sixty, recognized these qualities in his protégé and envisioned the day ten or fifteen years hence when Hasson would become his partner. But Hasson was in too much of a hurry to wait. At age twenty-seven, after an apprenticeship of two years, he went out on his own and founded the Augustus Hasson Literary Agency.

Hasson's early months were hard ones. Big-name writers weren't about to trust their fate to a neophyte hustler; and, without clients, an agent is nothing. Thus, face to face with reality, Hasson decided to nurture his own stable. Young authors, for whom Marcus Salinger and other superagents were off-limits, soon learned that a sympathetic ear was available. Hasson, in turn, weeded out the bad and kept the good. Then came his first book contracts, magazine installments, and payments on royalties—followed by one extraordinarily fortuitous event. Marcus Salinger's wife died and, in the month that followed, Salinger let slip the affairs of Leonard Wolfe, a young but already established author. In a fit of pique, Wolfe brought his account to Hasson, and Hasson, in turn, sold the novelist's next book to Random House for a lot of money. Soon, with the aid of some deft self-promotion, word got around that a new agent named Augustus Hasson was "picking money off the trees." By 1960 the majority of Marcus Salinger's former clients were doing business with Hasson, as were quite a few other name writers. By the time the "me decade" of the 1980s began, Augustus Hasson, at age fifty-one, was the hottest agent in publishing. Yet, unlike many of his contemporaries who expanded their staff and client lists to mammoth proportions, he kept his business pared to the bone. His clientele consisted of thirty or forty carefully chosen authors. His staff included one editorial assistant (female), a secretary, one messenger, and a "girl Friday." All business was conducted out of the East Side town house where Hasson worked and lived. He had become the most successful agent in the business. Or, as Big Walter explained on that long-ago night at Imbalzhno's, "Being agented by Augustus Hasson is like going surfing with The Beach Boys. You can't do any better."

Thus, there came into being a business as well as a social reason for my wanting to hear from Laura. Fortunately, the wait ended sooner rather than later. The morning after Big Walter and I had dinner at Imbalzhno's, the telephone rang and I was informed cheerfully by one Laura Kinney that she was (1) free for lunch, and (2) would be delighted to have the pleasure of my company.

Just before noon, we met at a bistro near Rockefeller Center.

"You're not the easiest person in the world to get in touch with," Laura told me as the maître d' led us to a table in back. "You're always out."

"Mostly in the library."

After we were seated, a waiter came and hovered nearby. Laura fiddled with the handle of her shopping bag from Saks until we'd ordered, then began the conversation: "What have you done all week?"

"Researched my book and thought about you."

If my answer struck a responsive chord, there was no sign of it.

"What about you?" I asked.

"I ate eggs."

"Pardon?"

"Eggs. Whenever I'm depressed, I lose my appetite and eat eggs. It's a throwback to my mother's feeding me breakfast before school when I was little." The same self-effacing smile I'd seen on two previous occasions touched her face. "In case you can't tell, my mental state is somewhat precarious."

Tentatively, I reached out to touch her hand, then thought better of it. For a moment, there was silence. Then, again, Laura was speaking.

"Actually, what happened is I've started realizing there's no way I can walk out of the marriage without leaving a large chunk of myself behind. For years, I've gone around thinking I made a mistake by marrying Allen, but the prospect of leaving conjures up an empty feeling in the pit of my stomach. I want to do it, but it's harder than I thought."

"What does Allen say on the subject?"

"He doesn't think I'm capable of leaving."

"And you?"

"I guess we'll find out. Allen and I haven't slept together for two weeks, which is a victory, of sorts. But whether I have the strength to leave—I suppose that's one of the reasons I wanted to see you. Somehow, you seem to give me strength."

A busboy appeared with rolls and water. I wasn't sure what to say next. All I knew was that this was a woman I was very attracted to on many levels, and that the territory was uncharted for both of us.

"How did you and Allen meet?" I asked at last.

Twisting her fingers, Laura creased her napkin before resting it in her lap. "Are you really interested?"

"Sure."

"It was a blind date. Allen was studying for the bar, and I'd just graduated from college. We went to the movies, and afterward he took me to Top of the Sixes for a drink."

"Is he the only person you've lived with?"

"Outside of college roommates, yes." Again the smile. "Actually, when we started living together, it was kind of nice. I'd been modeling for a while and gotten on a pretty fast track, which I didn't like."

"I didn't know you were a model."

Laura shrugged. "A lot of people have negative preconceptions about modeling. It's not something I brag about."

"How long did you do it?"

"Two years. In truth, I sort of fell into it. During my senior year of college, I went to a football game at Harvard. At halftime, a man came up to me and said he was vice-president of the Wilhelmina Agency in New York, gave me his card, and suggested I call Wilhelmina directly. After I graduated with a degree in sociology and no job, I figured what the heck.''

"And?''

"It had its moments. The first year, I made forty thousand dollars just being photographed; plus I got off on seeing myself in print. The second year, it went up to sixty thousand, but there were too many things about the job I didn't like. I'd become too preoccupied with what I was wearing and how I looked. There was no intellectual stimulation, and, since most models are in competition with one another, it was hard to develop friendships at work. That was one set of problems. Then I started worrying about the future. Modeling isn't exactly a long-term profession. Selling products is what it's about, and there's always a fresh supply of nineteen-year-olds who match your shoe size and eye color. No one keeps a model around for sentimental reasons, and I figured journalism or TV news was a more secure line of work. Beyond that, I wasn't happy with the life-style I'd fallen into. There were too many parties, and I was tired of the rich socialites who butterfly from one agency to the next. The whole thing was bringing out the worst in me, so I quit. Right after that, Allen and I started living together. He was a good roommate, and all the pressure of being single in Manhattan seemed to dissipate. I was tired of dealing with men who wouldn't take no for an answer, and living with Allen made it easy. I didn't have to worry about strangers and dates.''

"Until?''

"Very recently,'' she answered. "You have to understand, I'm from the school that believes marriages should be monogamous.''

The waiter returned, carrying our plates.

"I've got an idea,'' Laura said cheerfully. "Let's talk about something else.''

*   *   *

Lunch passed quickly, the food being ordinary but the company good. In addition to her other assets, Laura was smart, and I liked watching her mind work. At times she seemed incredibly disciplined, maybe even too organized for her own good. And then, suddenly, she'd come up with an off-the-wall idea, like sending Christmas cards in July, and I'd realize how much fun it was to be with her. There were so many things I wanted to ask, and, were the decision mine, we'd have talked for hours. But, as always, she had one eye on the clock.

"Do you want to take a walk?" I asked, still seated at the table when the meal was finished.

"I'd like to, but there are things I have to do before work."

Again, the dilemma—what to say next? An awkward question was building inside, and I had to ask it. "There's something I'd like to know," I said at last.

"Go ahead."

"I'm not quite sure how to ask this. I like you. I like you a lot. But I'm not clear—are we going to make love together again or not?"

There was a pause.

"Why don't we talk about it next time," Laura said.

"Does that mean I get to see you again?"

"Yes."

For the moment, at least, a heavy weight seemed to have lifted. Then I remembered my second reason for wanting to see Laura.

"There's something else," I said, a little apprehensive about mixing business with pleasure. "The day we met, you mentioned a literary agent named Augustus Hasson. I don't want to impose, but Big Walter told me about him, and, if you could arrange an introduction, I'd owe you a lot."

Again the smile; this time, understanding. "I know," she

answered. "In publishing, Augustus passes for royalty. Let me see what I can do about it."

Lunch was over. Reluctantly, I stood up and walked with Laura out to the street. Just short of the curb, she reached into her shopping bag and pulled out a small gift-wrapped box.

"Here," she said, thrusting it forward.

"For what?"

"It's a present, from Saks. Married women are always supposed to be generous with their lovers."

After lunch, my spirits were pretty good; enough so to consider taking the afternoon off. Then I decided to go down to the New York City Public Library for some research instead. "Life doesn't always come wrapped in nice neat little packages," I told myself in midafternoon as my thoughts drifted off to Laura. Around 4:30, I gave up trying to work and went home to go jogging with Big Walter. As usual, our course ran through Riverside Park.

"I don't think I could have an affair with a married woman," he said thoughtfully after I'd brought him up to date on the day's events.

"What if the woman came to you, and you were single?"

"Same answer—even if I liked her a lot. There are two things in life that strike me as wrong: extramarital sex and voting Republican."

After jogging, I ate dinner alone, then read. "Life can be complicated," I told myself. For whatever reason, I couldn't get Laura out of my head.

Just after 9:00, the house phone buzzed.

"Mr. Hammond," the doorman announced, "a young lady dropped off an envelope with your name on it."

"Is she still there?"

"No, sir. She handed it to me and left."

Somewhat apprehensive, I went down to the lobby and picked up the envelope, running it through my fingers on the elevator coming back up. "TOM HAMMOND," it said in clean block letters. In the sanctity of my apartment, I opened it:

Dear Tom,

I spoke with Augustus. Normally, he wouldn't be interested, but he and my father go back a long way, so he'll take a look.

Send him a letter, along with a short outline of your book. His address is 303 East 54th Street, N.Y. 10022. I'll be in touch.

Good luck!
Laura

P.S. If Augustus asks how we know each other, just tell him we met in the park.

5

May 15

Dear Mr. Hasson,

I'm writing at the suggestion of Laura Kinney, in the hope that you'll consider representing me in the sale of my novel.

By way of background information, until two weeks ago, I was an assistant professor of political science at Columbia. I intend to write full-time now and in the future.

Enclosed is the plot outline I plan to follow for my first book. I can be reached by telephone or at the address above, and look forward to hearing from you at your convenience.

Sincerely,
Thomas Hammond

*   *   *

"What do you think?" I asked Big Walter.
"Not bad. Let's see the plot."
I handed it over.

THE MARIAH PROJECT
by Thomas Hammond

David Barrett——American; tall, handsome, ruggedly athletic; just shy of forty; now working on special assignment for the CIA. Six years ago, his wife and infant son were killed in an automobile accident. Barrett is a man haunted by his past, groping for the future.

Carolyn Hewitt——Age twenty-seven; tall, sensuous, absolutely stunning; Ph.D. from the University of California at Berkeley; onetime chief research assistant to Ernest Reid (an American scientist employed by the Israeli government). Then Reid disappeared and Carolyn Hewitt was whisked away by the Israeli secret service.

Kaleel Rashad——Head of Intelligence for the Palestine Liberation Organization; trained by the Soviet KGB; financed by Libyan oil money. Rashad has assembled a team of assassins intent on locating Reid and destroying his work forever.

The Mariah Project is the story of a discovery that could turn the tide of civilization. For two years, Dr. Ernest Reid conducted ocean research, operating out of a battered ship that looked like a leaky shoe but contained the most sophisticated electronic equipment available. Reid was an oceanologist hired by the Israeli government to locate mineral deposits on the ocean floor. But somewhere in the South Pacific, he stumbled onto something more: a mother lode of complex crystals fashioned from a molecular chain, consisting of linked hydrogen and silicon (the principal ingredient of sand). When ignited, they yield an energy equivalent equal to 200 times that of concentrated oil.

Reid estimated his find at one trillion tons. But when he radioed word to an Israeli contact, he mentioned only the nature of his discovery, not its location. A young assistant was then dispatched on a small lifeboat with sample crystals intended for Jerusalem, but he never arrived. Instead, one week later, his bullet-riddled body washed up on a South Pacific island shore. Meanwhile, not knowing of the death, Reid brought his ship to Indonesia for supplies, where four more crewmen were murdered and the vessel destroyed in a raging fire. Soon after, the oceanologist fled, never to be found. Of his original staff, only Carolyn Hewitt (who was on leave at the time of the discovery) remains alive. After Reid's disappearance, she slipped into Jakarta and salvaged several crystals from the ship's remains on the harbor floor. Then, accompanied by Israeli secret-service agents, she brought them to Jerusalem. Thus the Israeli government has sample crystals. *But it doesn't know where in the Pacific they were found.*

Somewhere at the ocean bottom is an energy source more plentiful than all the oil known to man. In one fell swoop, the power of the Arab sheiks could be destroyed. But the Israeli government has to find Ernest Reid before Kaleel Rashad and his band of PLO assassins; and, toward that end, it asks for CIA aid. David Barrett and Carolyn Hewitt work hand-in-hand in a five-continent race against time.

Big Walter finished reading and put the outline aside. ''Congratulations,'' he murmured. ''It sounds like a winner.''

"Be honest."

"I am. It has all the elements of a blockbuster book; even the title is great." Warmth and sincerity were etched on his face. "Only one thing troubles me."

"What's that?"

"Will you still talk to me when you're rich and famous?"

"Big Walter, I'll make you a promise. If *The Mariah Project* becomes a best seller, you can write the screenplay for it."

Later that day, I mailed the outline to Augustus Hasson; then I went back to work. Over the weekend, I read several novels with an eye toward character development and plot. Sunday night, I had dinner with Big Walter and Patricia. Under their marital arrangement, it was Big Walter's turn to cook.

"Smells awful," I deadpanned as Patricia opened the door to their apartment. "What is it?"

"Liverwurst curry spread over a bed of lettuce and cold rice."

"That's totally false," Big Walter bellowed from the kitchen. "It's spaghetti with homemade pesto that happens to be very good."

"Well, hurry it up," Patricia grumbled. "Tom's probably hungry."

"Hurry it up," Big Walter mimicked, emerging from the kitchen. "Hurry it up! When William Shakespeare was writing *King Lear,* his wife did not say, 'William, hurry it up.' When Leonardo Da Vinci was painting *The Last Supper,* the models didn't whine, 'Finish it up, Leonardo, we're hungry.' " Snapping the tab off a can of beer, he slumped on the sofa. "Dinner will be ready when I feel like it."

"He's cranky," Patricia announced, turning toward me.

"So I see. What's the matter?"

"Yesterday he wrote a story, and I didn't like it."

If there's anything worse than getting caught in a fight between a husband and wife, it's getting caught in a fight between husband and wife over something the husband wrote. Instinctively, I wanted out, but Big Walter wouldn't hear of it. "All right," he demanded. "Let's let Tom be the judge."

"Fine," Patricia countered.

The conflict that unfolded was fairly straightforward. Big Walter had written a porn story about an aging rock-and-roll star. Now he wanted to sell it. "It's too raunchy for *Playboy* or *Penthouse,*" he admitted, "but *Gallery* might buy it."

"No!" Patricia pleaded. "Your writing is too important for you to lower yourself like that."

In due course, the offending exhibit was placed before the court. Evidence in hand, I began to read:

" 'His first wife had breasts like fried eggs . . .' "

In that vein, the story continued until a dramatic high point was reached: lyrics to the singer's smash rock hit:

> *I got an itchin' in my penis*
> *And it's gonna come between us*
> *'Cause, baby, I got VD*
>
> *Don't know where I caught it*
> *'Cause I know I never sought it*
> *But, baby, I got VD*

Then the narrative resumed, and the page ended on the following note:

*Things a Woman Should Never Say to a Man
When They're Making Love*

1. Can't you make it any bigger?
2. This better be good, or else.
3. My last lover had herpes.
4. Oh, my God! I forgot to put in my diaphragm.
5. Is that all?

"The truth is, it's a bit much," I said when I'd finished.

"It's a lot much," groused Patricia. "It's terrible. . . . Don't you understand," she said, turning to Big Walter, "I'm embarrassed for you. I love you, and I respect your writing too much to watch you do this to yourself."

"But there's nothing to be embarrassed about. I only wrote it for the money—money I can use to buy presents for you."

"I don't want presents. I just want you to tear it up. Please!"

Long pause.

Judge Hammond remained silent.

"She always gets what she wants through the imposition of guilt," Big Walter muttered. Then, with great drama, he lifted the pages on high and tore them in half, quarters, eighths, sixteenths, and on, until a mass of confetti littered the floor.

"The only reason I'm doing this," he grumbled, "is because I like it when you tell me you love me."

Monday and Tuesday, I went back to the library for more research. Wednesday, I read *The Devil's Alternative* by Frederick Forsyth. Thursday morning at 9:00, the telephone rang.

"Augustus Hasson would like to see you," a secretary said. "Please be here at ten o'clock tomorrow. . . . A.M.," she added.

*   *   *

What does one wear to make a good impression on a literary agent? As a general rule, I'm comfortable in jeans. Teaching class, I wore a sports jacket and slacks. For my first encounter with Augustus Hasson, I decided a suit was in order. Thus attired, I arrived at his East Side town house twenty minutes early. Not wanting to appear overanxious, I took a slow walk around the block. Then I returned and pressed the front-door buzzer. A cold-looking woman in her early thirties answered.

"I'm Marcia Steinberg, Mr. Hasson's editorial assistant," she announced. "You must be Thomas Hammond."

Something in her manner suggested that it might be appropriate to produce a driver's license or other form of identification.

"Come with me," she instructed.

Inside, we passed through a long corridor, which opened into a waiting room with several chairs, a sofa, and two desks. One of the desks was manned by a matronly looking woman of about forty, who was typing as though nothing else in the world mattered. The other was piled high with manuscripts of varying sizes.

"Mr. Hasson will be with you shortly," Ms. Steinberg advised. Then, without offering a seat, she disappeared into a small room to the right, closing the door behind her. Not quite sure what to do next, I stood by the sofa and looked around. The furniture was functional but undistinguished. The windowless walls were painted white. And, on the walls, was a remarkable sight: dust jackets—maybe two hundred of them—matted, mounted, and framed; each one from a bestselling book that Augustus Hasson had agented. *Two hundred best sellers.* Few publishing houses could boast of success like that.

The secretary kept typing. To satisfy my curiosity, I crossed to the vacant desk and glanced down at the pile of manuscripts. Beside them, a stack of postcards bearing the imprint of a form rejection message waited to be addressed.

Dear Author,

    Thank you for contacting me in connection with your work. Due to other commitments, I regret that I am unable to represent you.

Sincerely,
Augustus Hasson

Above the desk, the dust jacket from Augustus Hasson's most recent blockbuster hung triumphant: *Kennedy's Women* by Edwin Smyth—a book that devoted one chapter each to Judith Campbell Exner, Jayne Mansfield, Janet Leigh, and each of the other women John F. Kennedy reportedly had affairs with while he was in the White House. *Kennedy's Women* had sold 650,000 copies in hardcover and been number-one on *The New York Times* best-seller list for twenty weeks. Smyth was reported to be working on sequels about Bobby and Teddy.

The intercom on the secretary's desk sounded, and she stopped typing long enough to pick up the receiver. "Yes, Mr. Hasson. I'll send him in." Then, turning in my direction, she finally spoke: "Mr. Hasson will see you. His office is through the door straight ahead."

The man who would direct my future was sitting in a high-backed black leather chair behind an enormous chrome-and-glass-topped desk. Pale ash cabinets finished with highly polished Chinese lacquer lined the walls. A tall geometric brass sculpture stood on the floor. There were chairs and a window, but everything focused on the desk. Set eight or nine feet from the far wall, it consisted of a stylized base beneath a rectangular slab of glass, the edges of which shone green because of their density. For a man of Hasson's profession, the desktop itself was surprisingly bare. A large telephone with buttons indicating computer memory and four or five office extensions rested to the right. A few sheets of paper and several manuscripts sat piled beneath a Steuben glass paperweight. Everything was cold, modern, expensive, and highly impersonal—as though the decor had been chosen from a furniture-store catalog with the intent of precluding any imprint of a personal nature.

"Have a seat," Hasson ordered, making no effort to rise and greet me. His voice was deep, resonant and bass, carrying with it an aura of authority and self-assurance. At a guess, he was several inches shy of six feet, but it was hard to tell since he wasn't standing. His hair was thick black, combed back with sideburns trimmed high and just a touch of grey. As I'd expected, he was dressed impeccably: a dark grey suit and light blue shirt without the slightest wrinkle or smudge on his cuffs or collar.

Relieved that I hadn't worn jeans, I sat opposite the desk, choosing a chair that enabled me to catch sight of the area beyond the window. White vertical blinds partially obscured the view, but, even so, I could make out a well-landscaped garden beyond.

"I dine there," Hasson said, gesturing toward the garden. "There's a small table between the rose bushes and the fountain. Every morning, if the weather's nice, I have breakfast outdoors at seven. The same holds true for dinner—at a later hour, of course."

His face looked well-fed, possibly better than it should have been.

"Whenever possible, I arrange for luncheon engagements in the garden as well. I trust you'll forgive me for being immodest when I say that writers and editors respond quite favorably when invited to Augustus Hasson's for a business lunch. The food is excellent, and, among its other virtues, the arrangement saves me an enormous amount of time. Instead of losing forty minutes traveling to The Four Seasons and waiting for service, I simply step outside, and everything's there.''

The intercom buzzed and Hasson stabbed at a button, lifting the receiver. "Yes. . . . Tell him I'll call back in ten minutes." That done, he turned aside the top sheet on his pile of papers, and focused on several pages which I recognized as my outline for *The Mariah Project*.

"It's a good title," he said. "Very commercial. The plot is also quite good. Properly written, it has the potential to become a best seller, which is the only type of project that interests me. I have no affinity for journeyman authors."

I waited. After a pause, Hasson continued.

"As you're probably aware, I'm one of the more successful agents in the business. Each year, I ask four or five new authors to join me. By 'new,' you realize, I mean well-established writers who seek my support. I turn away forty of fifty would-be clients per week; that comes to several thousand rejections per annum. I'm speaking with you now partly because your plot outline indicates a certain talent, which separates you from most academics, and largely because you were referred to me by Laura Kinney. Hopefully, your book will be good and our relationship will become mutually beneficial. But first, let me tell you what not to expect.

"A literary agent is a business representative. As such, my main objectives are commercial. I will sell your book to a publisher, process your contract, and collect money from royalties due you. I am not—repeat *not*—the nurturing, hand-holding type. I'm not a midwife to the creative process. I cannot teach an incompetent how to write. I cannot sell an unsellable manuscript. I cannot solve any of my client's personal problems. And I choose not to lend money. If an author pesters me on any matter at any time, I drop him. That might sound harsh; but, in return, I deliver. Last year fourteen books sold more than 200,000 copies in hardcover. I agented five of them. Eighty-six books had a paperback run of a million or more. Twelve were mine. Do you have any questions?''

Five minutes had passed without my saying a word. Now, given the opportunity to speak, I was tongue-tied. ''What made you leave teaching?'' I'd expected Augustus Hasson to ask. And I was prepared to answer, ''I've read what's being published these days, and I'm as good.'' But, clearly, small talk and personal matters were out of place. And, in their stead, I was sitting like a dummy in front of the most successful agent in publishing.

''Do you want to see chapters as I write them?'' I asked finally.

''Absolutely not! The next time I hear from you should be when you send in the finished manuscript. If you have any questions along the way, relay them in the first instance to my assistant, Marcia Steinberg.''

''Yes, sir. I expect the book will be done in seven to eight months—a little after Christmas—if that's all right.''

''Take your time. There's no hurry.''

Leaning forward without rising from his chair, Augustus Hasson extended a hand, thus indicating that our meeting was over and forcing me to stand up in order to shake hands with him.

''Good luck,'' he said in a not-unfriendly voice. ''There are three things I look for in an author: ability, commitment, and personal style. I'm confident you'll do well on each count.'' As I reached the door on my way out, one final thought was uttered. ''By the way, my assistant said it was necessary to call five or six times before reaching you. You'd be well advised to purchase a telephone-answering machine if you plan on staying in the business.''

That night, I reported to Big Walter on publishing's premier agent.

"Take it from the beginning," he urged. "I want to hear all about him."

I started with Marcia Steinberg ("Thin face, thin ass, and too much gold jewelry"), then the physical layout of Augustus Hasson's office, and, finally, The Great One himself ("Clearly, his enthusiasm for books lies at the capitalistic end of the spectrum.").

"He sounds like a bastard," Big Walter said when I'd finished.

"You guessed it."

"But a powerful bastard. And he's on your side." Slowly, Big Walter's face brightened. "Hey! Congratulations! You've made it to the big time."

"Yeah. All I have to do now is write the book."

6

A T LEAST ONCE during the writing of a book, most authors doubt their ability to accomplish what they've set out to create. For over a year, I'd planned *The Mariah Project*. The plot and characters were set. A stack of index cards twelve inches high stood ready for use. But could I turn it all into a novel?

The day after I met with Augustus Hasson, I took the cards from their resting place on the bedroom shelf and thumbed through them:

Each cubic mile of seawater contains 165 tons of dissolved minerals—everything from table salt to gold.

Did Carolyn Hewitt have an affair with Ernest Reid? No! Her interest in the research project was purely scientific.

Most undersea mining explorations are government-run or backed by a consortium of multinational corporations.

Fragments—some connected to the main story, some not. Slowly, I spread the cards across my bedroom carpet, making little piles categorized by character, time sequence, and subject matter. Thousands of cards. What a mess! How was I ever going to turn them into a book?

"Don't worry about the rest of the novel," I decided. Concentrate on the start. Chapter One. What were my objectives? Introduce David Barrett; tell readers a little about the plot. Crawling around the carpet, I segregated the hundred-or-so cards that seemed relevant to the book's early scenes, returning the rest to their spot on the shelf. Then, per Augustus Hasson's instructions, I went out and bought a telephone-answering machine at a local appliance shop.

"I'm going to charge you for installing this," Big Walter advised after I'd discovered that my own mechanical abilities were insufficient to figure out the "easy two-step installation" promised by the instruction booklet. "It will cost you a brownie."

"Homemade or bakery bought?"

"Either way; it doesn't matter." Forty minutes later, the job was complete. "There you are," he announced. "Now you can faithfully receive all calls from Augustus Hasson."

The next day, I began to write. Several weeks earlier, I'd decided to do the bulk of my work away from home. There were too many distractions in the apartment (stereo, refrigerator, telephone, and TV, to name a few). Also, I was afraid that spending too many hours at home would leave me isolated and depressed. My first thought had been to write at Columbia, but that was a forty-minute walk. Then I'd considered the library at Lincoln Center, but the hours were too short. Finally, I'd discovered Fordham Law School, which seemed ideal for my purposes. The school was located one block south of Lincoln Center at 62nd Street. Formal library hours were limited, but the main reading room was available to students and alumni on a round-the-clock basis. The lighting was good and chairs comfortable. Users could choose between long wood-grained tables on the library's ground floor and individual cubicles on a balcony level. The only drawback I could see concerned an imposing sign on the library door, which decreed: "EVERYONE—STUDENTS, FACULTY, AND STAFF—MUST PRESENT A CURRENT FORDHAM IDENTIFICATION CARD BEFORE BEING ADMITTED TO THE LIBRARY." Now, on my first day of actual writing, the Fordham security network was about to be tested. Approaching the guard on duty, I smiled with a modicum of trepidation and inquired, "How are you today?"

"Fair to middlin'," he answered as I walked by unobstructed.

The library itself was almost empty because of the summer recess. Taking a seat at a table in back, I opened my attaché case and extracted the tools of my trade: a yellow pad, Chapter One index cards, a ball-point pen, *Roget's Thesaurus*. Then I sat back and looked around. The room was enormous; maybe thirty yards long and two-thirds as wide. Four rows of tables (twelve per row) stretched from one end to the other. Plate-glass windows covered the entire east wall, which was at least twenty feet high. The carpet was industrial orange. Endless rows of legal texts were massed on shelves beneath the balcony level.

"Okay, Hammond!" I told myself. "Get to work." Not certain what to do next, I picked up my pen and stared at the lined yellow pad in front of me. I needed a first sentence:

He lay flat on the brown pine-needled floor of the forest.

Hemingway! That was what came to mind. . . . How about Steinbeck:

To the red country and part of the grey country of Oklahoma, the last rains came gently.

Or maybe Homer:

Sing, Goddess, the anger of Peleus' son Achilles.

"Let's go, Hammond. Your career's on the line."

David Barrett . . .

David Barrett looked up at the threatening sky . . .

Cross it out; start over.

The threatening sky . . .

"Hammond, whatever made you think you could write?"

The ominous sky hung heavy overhead as David Barrett . . .

"That's better! Keep going!"

I wrote until 5:00, then packed up and went over to see Big Walter, who was mopping the building steps when I arrived.

"Mrs. Weinberg is in the hospital," he announced. (Mrs. Weinberg was an eighty-year-old tenant in the building who was second only to Patricia in complaining about the occasional lack of hot water.)

"What happened?"

"You won't believe it." Laying the mop aside, he wiped his forehead and settled on the top step. "This morning, Mrs. Weinberg's daughter called me and said Mrs. Weinberg hadn't answered the phone since yesterday. The family was getting worried and wanted me to go upstairs to check her out. So I went up, knocked on the door, and asked, 'Mrs. Weinberg, is everything all right?' And from inside, she answered, 'Who wants to know?' " Shaking his head, Big Walter continued. "Anyway, I recognized the voice, figured everything was fine, and went downstairs to call the daughter. Then, about an hour later, I realized Mrs. Weinberg hadn't given me a direct answer. So I went back upstairs, knocked on the door again, and this time there was no answer. I took my passkey, went inside, and there's Mrs. Weinberg, lying on the floor with a broken hip—from a fall last night."

"You're kidding!"

"No, I'm not. A broken hip, and, before she'll tell anybody, she wants to know who's asking. She'd been on the floor for sixteen hours."

Wearily, Big Walter picked up his mop and began to scrub. "That was the day's major event. On a lesser note, I forgot to take the Kleenex out of my pajama pocket when I did the laundry. Patricia will kill me when she gets home from work. There's shredded Kleenex all over the wash."

"Anything else?"

"Yeah, I talked to an agent—someone my sister dredged up last week at a party."

"That's great," I said, hoping to make Big Walter a little more enthusiastic.

"Right! Fantastic! This agent does business out of the Bagel Nosh Deli on Broadway and 70th Street. She sits at a table by the front window. Prior to her present job, she worked as a waitress at Lüchow's. I asked how come she became a literary agent and she told me, 'Mr. Walker, I became an agent because Jesus wanted it for me.' Then she launched into a ten-minute spiel on the virtues of Reverend Jerry Falwell, which ended when I got up and left." His job done, Big Walter twirled the mop over his shoulder and started up the steps. "Write down that story about Mrs. Weinberg on a piece of lined yellow paper," he suggested. "You can use it someday in a book."

Ignoring the advice, I went home and checked the answering machine for messages (there were none), then went jogging alone in the park. Physically, I felt pretty good, and, at a guess, I ran four or five miles. Then I ate some shrimp with lobster sauce from a nearby Chinese restaurant, and reread what I'd written earlier in the day on my book.

Shortly before midnight, the telephone rang and things livened up a bit.

"Let's take a walk in Central Park tomorrow," Laura said.

We met the following afternoon at the statue of Daniel Webster, just inside the park at 72nd Street. Laura was wearing a dark blue suit—the first time I'd seen her in "business dress." As always, she was groomed to perfection— a concession possibly to her earlier days as a model for Wilhelmina.

"Augustus called last night to say that the two of you had a nice conversation. He was very impressed."

"How could he be impressed? I didn't say anything."

"That's what he liked. To his way of thinking, you were appropriately deferential and businesslike."

Thankful for small favors, I tried to imagine how The Great One might have described our meeting to Laura. A couple of kids with skateboards rolled by. The sky was blue overhead.

"I'd like to talk," Laura said. "Could we find a place to sit?"

Looking for a sign of what was coming, I led the way to a nearby bench.

"All right," Laura continued, interrupting my thoughts. "As usual, I guess I'll start. . . . Allen is in Atlanta on business this week, and, when I called last night, I thought his being away would make seeing you easier. I even harbored the idea of going back to your apartment and going to bed. This morning I started having second thoughts. The truth is, Allen's a very sweet person, and, for all his faults, he loves me. My leaving is causing him more pain than I imagined. I want to leave. I'm going to leave. But, until I do, it's wrong for me to have an affair with you, or anyone else." Somewhere, not too far beneath the surface, Laura was struggling to maintain her composure. "I'm sorry to be so erratic. But, until I straighten out my life, I really can't see you."

"I'm not quite sure I understand."

"What I'm saying is, I'm not strong enough emotionally to handle a relationship with you, romantic or platonic. Leaving Allen is the hardest thing I've ever done, and trying to incorporate you into my life makes it harder. I've already got more guilt than I can handle, and I'm not about to substitute you for Allen. Try to understand, please!"

"Maybe you should try a little to understand. I have feelings, too—or haven't you noticed?"

"I've noticed, Tom. But, right now, your feelings aren't like mine. Right now I'm as unhappy as I've ever been in my life. There's an empty feeling inside me, and I don't know what if anything is left. In the middle of the night, I wake up, and the first thing I think of is I have to get away from this man and this marriage. Then I look past the bedroom door into the living room, and Allen is sitting on the edge of the sofa, staring at our wedding album, sobbing. One minute, the thought of his touching me shoots revulsion all through my body. The next, I realize what my leaving means to him, and I wonder how I can do this to someone I used to love.''

"I thought you'd already made that decision.''

"Yes, Tom. I've made that decision—and I'll stick by it. I'll take the pain in as part of life. But, in the meantime, I don't need people pretending to be understanding when they're not.'' Her voice began to rise. "And I'm sick and tired of people who give exactly what they want to give and don't give a damn about anyone but themselves. I get it at home; I get it at work. I don't need it from you, too. And if those sentiments piss you off, I don't care. You can believe exactly what you want to believe about me because, in the end, that's what people do anyway.''

Almost frenetically, she grabbed at her purse as though readying to leave, then sank back down on the bench.

"Tom,'' she said softly, touching her forehead with a hand. "Tom, I'm sorry. I'm acting like a crazy woman.''

The anger was gone. Laura looked toward me.

"Tom, you have to understand. This is my life, and I don't know what I've gotten into. It's tearing me apart.''

Her voice was barely audible.

"Yesterday morning . . . before Allen left for Atlanta, he wanted to kiss me. I didn't want it, but I figured he'd be gone for five days, so I gave him a kiss. And then all morning I felt dirty—not because I'd kissed him, but because I was being so fucking cruel that I begrudged him one goddamn lousy kiss.''

"It wasn't cruel.''

"Yes, it was. It was cruel, and I knew it. And then, I told him my leaving was a wound that would heal, and he said, 'No, it was an amputation,' and maybe he'd be able to live without me and maybe he wouldn't. . . . Don't you see? I can't cope with a lover. What I need desperately now is a friend; and the way you and I began, you can't be my friend.''

Her hands were taut, clutching at the air like a drowning person grasping at water. Then, suddenly——

''Tom, good-bye. I'll call you someday and tell you what happened, when it's over.''

''Why does it have to be this way?''

Then Laura Kinney stood up and walked off without looking back. And I was left sitting alone on a bench in Central Park with the realization that, most likely, I'd never see her again.

One afternoon in my apartment was really all it had been.

7

THAT NIGHT, I went over to visit Big Walter and Patricia. Patricia was making a cheesecake for a friend's birthday party. Big Walter was vacuuming the apartment, and seemed pleased by my arrival because it gave him an excuse to stop.

"Do you think Laura will leave her husband?" he asked when I'd finished my postmortem on the day's events.

"I don't know. Part of her wants to. Part of her doesn't. Right now, she paints a pretty bleak picture of being married; but they've been together for six years, so there must have been something right."

"Which leaves us with what?"

"I don't know about you, but I need a girlfriend. All my friends are married, half of them are having babies, and I can't even get a date."

"Don't worry about it," Big Walter counseled. "Someday

you'll find a nice career woman who's tired of coming home and eating TV dinners in a dirty studio apartment. You cook, you clean, and, now that you're writing, you're even home during the day to take care of children. You're a marvelous catch."

Acknowledging the compliment with a shrug, I reached for the beer that Patricia offered.

"You and Big Walter could try the zoo again," she suggested. "Or you could hang around the Plaza Hotel, which is where we met."

"The Plaza?"

"Outside it, actually," Big Walter said. "Before I got the job as building super, I had a vending cart on Central Park South. To drum up business, I'd stand on the curb opposite the Plaza and sing old rock-and-roll hits. One night Patricia and a friend walked by, and I offered them a free ice cream sandwich."

Somehow the vision of Big Walter singing "Don't Be Cruel" was rather amusing—except I couldn't help feeling sorry for guests at the Plaza.

"It's true," Patricia said, picking up where her husband had left off. "I didn't want to eat it, but my friend Melody made me. Then Big Walter talked with us for about an hour and asked me for a date."

"And?"

"We went to the movies, and he was a perfect gentleman. Next, on our second date, he invited me to his apartment for dinner. Everything was fine that time, too, except, when I arrived, he was watching professional wrestling on television. Some guy nicknamed The Vanilla Gorilla was stomping a three hundred–pound black Baptist minister named The Blesser. After that, I invited him to my place for shrimp creole a la Patricia. That's when I learned he was a pervert. Instead of bringing wine or flowers, he showed up with a box from Lord & Taylor's. I opened it up, and inside were a bra and panties.''

"More original than flowers," Big Walter interrupted.

"Anyway," Patricia continued, "he gave me the bra and panties on our third date. Now, keep in mind, at this point I'm starting to like him, but he hasn't touched me yet. And those were the days when people jumped into bed together pretty quickly. Then, a few nights later, he invited me to his apartment to watch 'Monday Night Football' on ABC. So I go over and all the big dummy does is watch football, and maybe he kisses me once or twice during commercials before the game ends at midnight. Then he starts putting on his coat to walk me home, at which point I grabbed him and very politely said, 'Take me to bed, you idiot.' "

"It didn't really happen that way, did it?'' I asked.

Looking a bit nostalgic, Big Walter nodded. "The truth is, I liked this woman more than anyone I'd ever met, and I was scared stiff that somehow I'd blow it. It wasn't until we actually got married and were halfway through our honeymoon that I stopped worrying about losing her."

"And after the honeymoon, you lived happily ever after,'' I concluded.

"With occasional problems," Patricia added. "Marriage is hard, Tom. It's not all fun and games. It takes trade-offs and a lot of hard work. Someday you'll see."

The next morning, I went back to Fordham to work on my book. In truth, the "plot outline" I'd sent to Augustus Hasson wasn't an outline, but a preface: something akin to dust-jacket copy designed to engender interest. The novel itself began chronologically after Ernest Reid's disappearance, and the character it focused on most was David Barrett.

At first glance, Barrett was the strong, silent type, but the person I hoped to create was quite complex. It wasn't enough for me to tell readers that he was tall, handsome, and worked

as a CIA agent. I had to fill him out with emotions and
personal quirks.

Sitting at a table by the library window, I began the task of
molding my character: birthplace, age, appearance, job. Barrett was a likable sort, far less macho than the customary CIA
hero most readers would expect. His motivation? Love of
country and excitement; plus working for the CIA paid the
bills. But, nearing age forty, with his wife and child dead,
David Barrett was burning out. The Mariah Project would
be his last case, and everybody associated with the agency
knew it.

Write a sentence. . . . Cross it out. . . . Change a word. . . .
Smooth things over. . . . Barrett was in a conference room
with Creighton Davis, the CIA's Director of Operations:

> Davis waited until the secretary had left, then opened
> his hand and held out an irregularly shaped crystal that
> looked very much like rock candy. "This crystal,"
> Davis began, "was formed from sand. Some unknown
> process, perhaps even before the ocean was formed,
> caused it to happen.
>
> Barrett waited, and the Director continued.
>
> "Over the years, tribal myths hinted at the existence
> of an unknown energy source somewhere in the South
> Pacific, but our analysts never took the reports seri-
> ously. Now we're believers." Placing the crystal on the
> table between them, Davis reached into a vest pocket and
> took out a small jeweler's pick. Barrett looked on as the
> Director chipped at the crystal until a tiny sliver, less than
> an eighth of an inch in diameter, sprang loose and tumbled
> onto a brass plate. Davis struck a match and leaned for-
> ward. The crystal flared, then began to burn with a high,
> steady flame. "This chip weighs approximately one-tenth

of a gram. It will burn for twelve hours. A large sector of the ocean floor—perhaps an area the size of Texas— is paved with them. They're there for the taking.''

"What's the catch?''

"The catch, Barrett, is that twelve men have been murdered trying to find out where these crystals came from. And we still don't know the answer.''

As the week passed, I buried myself in *The Mariah Project*. David Barrett accepted his assignment and flew to Jerusalem for further briefing. Meanwhile, spurred on by my own enthusiasm, Big Walter made substantial progress in revising a screenplay he'd written a year earlier. Then, in a mood of optimism, he mailed out a dozen copies of two previous scripts—no mean commitment, considering the postage and duplicating costs involved.

"There's nothing worse than an unsold manuscript,'' he confided to me that night. "It's like a dead fish wrapped in newspaper that's been lying around the house for weeks. No matter what, I have to keep trying. A writer can't give up.''

The weekend came and went without incident. A short note from Laura, apologizing for her ''outburst,'' arrived in the mail: "It seems as if I'm always apologizing,'' she wrote. "*Please* don't try to get in touch. Your offer of friendship is much appreciated, but, for the time being at least, I'm best off alone.''

Reluctantly, I concluded that our romance was at an end. The realization hurt, and, when I admitted as much, Big Walter offered a modicum of consolation: "Look at the bright side,'' he counseled. "At least you can say you never knowingly made love with a married woman.''

With Laura gone, I grew more engrossed in the book. The Fordham library became my office; David Barrett became my friend. Midway through the second week, I sensed *The Mariah Project* coming alive. I could feel myself talking with Israeli intelligence agents in Jerusalem. David Barrett began to reject dialogue I'd planned for him and spoke his own mind. All signs were positive. Even a message received in the mail from Augustus Hasson was cause for encouragement:

> Dear Tom,
>
> Please take note of the accompanying advice, drawn from my many years' experience in publishing.
>
> I look forward to reviewing your manuscript upon completion.
>
> > Sincerely,
> > *Augustus Hasson*

The signature, wholly illegible, bore some resemblance to an "A" and an "H" scrawled beside one another. Clipped to the letter was a mimeographed sheet headed "Rules for Novels":

1. A novel needs a main character. The character must be real—fleshed out with personal and biographical data (everything from college degrees to lines on his or her face). That character should be sympathetic. In a good book, the main character comes face to face with life and is changed.

2. A novel needs a framework/format/vehicle that will pull the story together and place it in focus. A series of disjointed chapters won't work.

3. A reader has to care about what happens to the main character. There must be a sense of tension and action—a reason to turn the page.

4. A book needs a setting, be it a Wall Street law office or a village in Africa. Certain objects (a parquet floor, a thatched hut) must be shown.

5. Take your time. Use a high standard of care. If a word, sentence, or paragraph sounds wrong, it doesn't belong—do it again. High-quality transitional paragraphs are often the hardest to construct.

Studying "Hasson's Laws," I compared them to my own plans for *The Mariah Project*. On each count, I'd followed his advice.

June arrived, without further word from Laura. With David Barrett fairly well developed as a character, I began to focus more on PLO–assassin Kaleel Rashad. Another week passed in the Fordham library and on Friday, to celebrate a particularly good half-day's work, I decided to quit early and go jogging.

"Come on over," Big Walter said when I telephoned for a companion. "I'll join you as soon as I finish a few things around the apartment."

Dressed in jogging shoes and cut-offs, I went by a little before 4:30 and found Big Walter on the working end of a vacuum cleaner.

"I thought you did that last week," I shouted over the roar of the Electrolux.

"So did I. But Patricia reminded me that, when you got here, I stopped. Last night she lay down the law: vacuum the apartment or else."

"Or else what?"

"I don't know, but I'm not particularly anxious to find out. Patricia can't sleep at night if there are dishes in the sink. She rinses paper plates before throwing them in the garbage. You can imagine what it does to her psyche when the apartment is dirty.'' Twenty minutes later, the job was complete. "Now all I have to do is empty the garbage," Big Walter announced.

"Hurry it up. I want to go jogging before midnight."

The responsive look was more bemused than obedient. Then, rubbing his nose, Big Walter trudged extra slowly into the kitchen to extract a garbage-filled bag from beneath the sink. "You know something," he grumbled. "If you and Patricia have your way, my tombstone will read, 'Hurry up, Big Walter; hurry up.' "

Around 5:30 (the same time as always), we finally got to Riverside Park. Most of the benches on the promenade were empty. The 83rd Street playground was filled with kids. A gentle breeze blew up from the river, making the weather ideal for jogging. Buoyed by the conditions, we ran north to 120th Street, then started back.

"I've been thinking," Big Walter reported.

"And?"

"And I've decided that, once every ten years, all corporate executives should be sent to jail for six months on the theory that they must have done something to deserve it."

"What about politicians?"

"Politicians, too; but to change the subject, I'd like your advice on a screenplay I'm writing."

"Be my guest."

For the next few minutes, we tossed about various visual images and plot twists. At one point, at Big Walter's request, I took my pen out and jotted down a note so he wouldn't forget "the best idea" he'd had all week.

"How's The Great American Novel coming?" he asked as the conversation progressed.

"Pretty good. There were times this week when sitting in

the library was like going to the movies. Fantasizing for eight hours a day isn't a bad way to earn a living.''

Off to the right, a group of grade-school children were playing soccer. In the distance, a woman jogger dressed in white shorts and a blue shirt had come into view and was moving toward us.

"I know the feeling," Big Walter said. "At least, the fantasizing part. The part about earning a living is unfamiliar turf.''

"Don't worry. You'll make it.''

"That's what I keep telling myself. But sometimes I get the sense that— Oh, Jesus! Over there—look!''

Ten yards ahead, the approaching jogger was in full view. Never in my life had I seen a woman so gorgeous. I mean it. This was the most incredible-looking being God ever created. Piercing blue eyes, bright, with a blazing crystalline clarity; shoulder-length brown hair, with glints that danced in the sunlight; a figure that outstripped the imagination of Vargas; a warmth and glow that bordered on mythological.

Big Walter and I stopped dead in our tracks, blinded by the light.

"Oh, my God,'' I whispered.

Running hard, The Ultimate Woman was already past us.

"Do something. . . . Anything. . . . Can't——''

"Don't talk,'' Big Walter ordered. "Just catch her. . . . Go!''

I began to run, without any real sense of why or what I'd do or say if I caught up to her. . . . Thirty yards . . . Twenty . . . The distance between us narrowed. Finally, near the northern tip of the park, she looped back and I pulled even.

"Hello!''

A bit startled, she looked toward me. Her hair hung like strands of gold. The ample curve of her breasts rose and fell beneath her pale blue cotton shirt. Everything about her was flawless, from her white jogging shoes to the terrycloth sweatband that held her hair in place—except it suddenly occurred to me that I had chased after her like a breathless lunatic, and she was probably getting ready to scream, "Help! Police!"

"Are you a regular runner?" I managed to gasp.

She smiled! A bit guarded, but what a smile! If this woman had been around in Renaissance times, every museum in Europe would——

"An irregular regular," she answered without breaking stride. "Two or three times a week."

She was perfect. Absolutely one hundred percent perfect—her voice, her manner.

"What do you do for a living?"

"I'm a writer," she said.

"No kidding! I'm——"

"I turn off here," she interrupted, cutting to the left. "Have a good run. Maybe I'll see you again in the park."

Big Walter was waiting for me just north of 80th Street.

"How'd it go?" he demanded.

"I'm in love."

"Congratulations. What's her name?"

"I don't know yet." Glossing over the futility of my cause, I tried to explain: "Big Walter, did you ever just want to go up to someone, touch hands, and never let go? It's crazy; I know it. I don't know her name. But I feel like I've been waiting for this woman all my life."

"Let's not get carried away. Good looks do not a person make."

"It's more than looks. It's everything. In all my fantasies, all my dreams, I've never seen anyone like her."

Ever so slowly, Big Walter pondered my mental state.

"All right," he said, gazing skyward. "In honor of your fixation, we'll call her The Fantasy Jogger."

"Couldn't you come up with something a bit less ridiculous?"

"To the contrary, I think The Fantasy Jogger sounds just right."

That night, for whatever reason, I felt particularly lonely. Maybe it was the prospect of Friday and Saturday without a date. Maybe it was the loss of whatever might have been with Laura.

Big Walter and Patricia were at the movies. I dialed a few other numbers, but no one was home.

She'd smiled at me. This afternoon in the park, The Fantasy Jogger had smiled. Either she liked me, or she was incredibly nice—or both.

Most of the evening lay ahead. There was nothing much on television to watch.

If I could choose anything in the world to be doing right now, it would be sitting here with her. I should have kept the conversation going. Somehow, I could have done it.

Why was I fixating like this? Maybe it was Laura; or the solitary nature of writing—or something more. . . . Pen in hand, I moved to my desk. Do it now! Don't wait!

The plane touched down on the Jakarta runway. David Barrett rubbed his eyes and fought to clear his mind. Four days of briefing in Jerusalem had taken their toll. . . .

Keep going! Don't stop!

The clock on my desk touched midnight. Local agents met Barrett at the airport and whisked him away to the Israeli Embassy compound.

One A.M. . . . One-thirty . . . Outside my bedroom window, the streets were empty. The seconds ticked by:

"There's not much else to tell you, Barrett. From this point on, the full resources of the American and Israeli governments are at your command—money, manpower; just ask and it's yours. Ernest Reid's chief research assistant, Carolyn Hewitt, will be working with you. She's waiting now at the hotel."

The moment had come. Carolyn Hewitt, who would be a part of my life for as long as *The Mariah Project* remained unfinished, was on the verge of creation. She would be warm and beautiful, brilliant and kind. Very soon, she and David Barrett would fall in love. She and The Fantasy Jogger were one.

Thus are obsessions born.

PART
TWO

8

J UNE AND JULY melted together as my work schedule became routine. Each day I woke up at 8:00, shaved, showered, ate breakfast, ran errands, and got to the library by 11:00. For the next six hours, I'd write—usually with a fifteen-minute break in midafternoon. Then, sometime around 5:00, I'd pack up and go jogging. The Fantasy Jogger failed to reappear, although more than once I charted my run to maximize a sighting. Whoever she was, wherever she was, I couldn't find her.

Overall, I enjoyed the summer. It was exciting to sit back and watch *The Mariah Project* unfold. Some days, I'd shut my eyes and actually see the star-studded South Pacific sky. At all hours of the day and night, characters I'd created would pop up, pound on my brain, and holler, "I have something to say; get a pen and write it down." David Barrett was the creation I identified with most, but the one closest to my heart was Carolyn Hewitt. She was the embodiment of perfection, and, through my writing, both character and role model had come alive. In the library, at home, constantly, I thought of her. More than once, I was moved to reflect on the Chinese philosopher Chuang-Tzu, who confounded generations by writing of a dream that he was a butterfly playing in the sun—and when he awoke, he wasn't sure whether he was Chuang-Tzu who had dreamt he was a butterfly, or a butterfly dreaming that it was the philosopher Chuang-Tzu. That's how real Carolyn Hewitt had become:

> The hot summer air hung heavy above. The glow of a thousand stars reflected in her eyes. She had the courage to say it first, which was one of the things Barrett liked most about her: "I've never felt this way before. Are we falling in love?"

One afternoon—a bit mystified, maybe even troubled, by the intensity of my emotional involvement—I confided in Big Walter.

"Don't worry about it," he counseled. "Everyone needs a fantasy life. And believe me, after eight years of failure, I'm an expert on the subject. I've constructed an entire world of Academy Awards and half-million-dollar advances. There are times when that and Patricia are all that keep me going.

The following morning, I went back to the library and continued writing. David Barrett and Carolyn Hewitt left the South Pacific together, their passion cataloged in scenes that transformed The Fantasy Jogger into my lover, companion, and friend. I touched her lips, kissed her, felt her body against mine. One afternoon I tried writing in the park, mindful of the possibility that she might pass by. She didn't. And at day's end, feeling silly and self-conscious, I looked back over my meager work product and vowed not to commit that particular folly again. But that night, more lonely and vulnerable than I cared to admit, I picked up the Manhattan telephone directory and thumbed through it.

"Fantasy Travel . . . Fantasy Ltd." Bemused, I noted that there was no entry under "Fantasy Jogger." Maybe I should look under "T" or "J"—no entry there, either. Turning the pages, I thought back to women I'd known years earlier; in college and after; lovers and friends. Some had brought out the best in me; others hadn't.

"Kinney, Carol . . . Kinney, Donna." There was no directory entry under "Kinney, Laura." . . . Several under "Kinney, L.," but more likely the phone was listed under Allen's name . . . "Kinney, Allen; 311 East 64th Street." That would be it; but Laura worked nights. . . . There it was: "National Broadcasting Company, 30 Rockefeller Plaza, 664–4444." . . . Maybe I should call and leave a message; or better yet, I could write. A simple handwritten note that Laura could answer or ignore as she saw fit. I wasn't quite sure why I was doing it, other than the fact that I was lonely. But a note would be fair, and reasonably unintrusive.

Pen in hand (and wary of the fact that letters to the office are far from private) I began to write:

Dear Ms. Kinney,

It's been quite a while since we discussed the difficulties inherent in transferring videotape from Libya to New York. If you have a moment, I'd love to hear from you on the subject.

Sincerely,
Thomas Hammond

June passed without a response. Meanwhile Patricia got a twenty-dollar-a-week raise just before her boss flew off to

Europe. And Big Walter started receiving rejections on the screenplays he'd submitted. "Dear Mr. Walker," read a typical note. "Thank you for your interest, but our studio does not read unsolicited manuscripts." . . . "Dear Mr. Walker," began another. "Thank you for writing. Unfortunately, your screenplay is not suited to our needs." Some producers returned the screenplay with their rejection letter. Others didn't, oblivious to the fact that each copy had cost $12 to Xerox.

"The Universal Studios rejection was particularly galling," Big Walter reported one afternoon while we were jogging in the park. "The first twenty pages were crumpled at the edges and the rest of the manuscript hadn't been touched. After page twenty, the reader inserted a book of matches to indicate where he'd left off. The matches actually came back with the screenplay."

"Maybe you could use them for something constructive," I suggested. "Like firebombing Universal's New York office."

Later in the week, Big Walter's screenplays elicited two more rejection letters. Meanwhile, *Time* magazine reported that Augustus Hasson had sold rights to *RFK's Women* for an advance of $1.5 million and engineered the sale of "a major diet book" for $600,000. Each day, I checked my telephone answering machine, but there was no message from Laura and few of consequence from anyone else. Perhaps the most creative tiding came from Big Walter, whose voice-on-tape greeted me one afternoon when I returned home from writing: "This country is insane," he stated. "I called three people today and got three telephone-answering machines."

By late July, the first six chapters of *The Mariah Project* were complete. Rather than wait until the novel was finished, I hired a typist, who (for a dollar a page) transformed my burgeoning pile of yellow paper into ninety typed pages. One week later, she returned the manuscript. "It's good," she said. "I'm anxious to see what happens next."

That night, to celebrate my first favorable review, I went out for dinner with Big Walter and Patricia. Afterward, we returned to their apartment to play Monopoly. Normally, I'm not excited by board games, but this one had a special twist. Fate was in Big Walter's pocket. Before the game was an hour old, he owned half the board and was rolling dice as if there was no tomorrow. Meanwhile, I was struggling on the edge of bankruptcy, and the only decent properties Patricia owned were Pennsylvania and Pacific Avenues. So what happened? Big Walter *gave* her North Carolina Avenue in exchange for a jelly donut, after which Patricia bought three hotels by stealing money from the bank and wiped us both out.

"It's your fault," she said when the game was over and she confessed her theft. "You should have paid closer attention to what I was doing."

"But you're my wife!" wailed Big Walter. "Stealing from Tom, I can understand; cheating your own husband is awful."

The debate continued until Patricia agreed to a "forfeit in principle." Big Walter was declared "The Monopoly Winner" and, cheered by the prospect of "peace in our time," I went home to bed. The following morning, I got up, shaved, showered, and checked the mail on my way out to do errands. Mixed in with fund solicitations from Norman Lear and the American Wilderness Society was a plain white envelope bearing the NBC logo. Opening it up, I stared down at Laura's neatly clipped handwriting:

Dear Tom,

How long has it been since we've seen each other? Six weeks, I think. The truth is, I was glad to get your letter. Just knowing you're out there makes me feel better.

Allen and I are about where you left us. He suggested marriage counseling; I refused. I suggested a trial separation; he said no. So-o-o, the burden is on my shoulders, which is where it was the day you and I met. The whole experience is unspeakably painful, but I've just about gathered the courage to go look for an apartment.

By the way, I didn't know you were interested in shipping videotape from Libya. Call me at work some night after midnight and maybe we can arrange a get-together on the subject.

Fondly,
Laura

We met two days later in Riverside Park. As usual, Laura was dressed impeccably, though her face seemed a bit thinner than the last time I'd seen her.

"It's from not sleeping," she confided as we made our way along the river. "All my life, I've been able to put my head on a pillow and go to sleep. That's a hard thing to give up."

"Have you tried a sedative?"

"I will if I have to, but I'd rather not."

For thirty minutes or so, we talked about the same things as always: Allen, broken marriages, divorce, and the like. Then, gradually, we moved to happier subjects.

"How's your friend?" Laura asked. "The one who introduced us in Central Park?"

"Big Walter? He's fine. In fact, he told me to send you his best."

"Is he really as sweet as he seemed the day we met?"

"Absolutely, yes."

Two sailboats were near the water's edge. For a while, we watched them tacking back and forth, then decided to walk over to 78th Street to see if Big Walter wanted to join us. He did—and we returned to Riverside Park as a threesome.

"You know something," he opined as the conversation progressed. "Having me along is highly appropriate. After all, I was responsible for the start of this relationship."

In time, we made our way north to the playground at 83rd Street, where Laura suggested we ride the swings.

"You've got to be kidding," Big Walter moaned. "I weigh too much."

With considerable coaxing, we got him to go first. Then came my turn; and, finally, Laura's—her hair flowing up in a self-created breeze as she arched toward the sky. Then we returned to meandering. A few children on bicycles passed nearby. Big Walter fingered the hole in the elbow of his green-and-white striped shirt. Laura seemed more relaxed than earlier in the day, and it showed in her face.

"Do you remember your dreams?" she asked, addressing the question to Big Walter.

"Sometimes."

"Are they in color or black and white?"

"I don't know. Both, I guess."

We tossed that idea around for a while, then began comparing notes from childhood. "When I was four," Laura said, "I buried my entire marble collection in the garden. I thought it would grow marble trees during the summer."

"I played football in high school," Big Walter reminisced, "and hated every minute of it. The coach wanted me to smash people, and everybody was about half my size. I always felt sorry for the other side. Finally, after about a month, the coach decided there was no room on the squad for a passive offensive tackle, and he let me quit."

The trail dipped down to the river, then climbed back to the promenade overlooking the Hudson. The late-afternoon sun was warm and bright. We walked with Big Walter on the right, Laura between us. Just beyond 98th Street, there was a turn in the path. "If you want a true view of American culture," Big Walter was saying, "don't read Alistair Cooke or Kenneth Clark. Read sixty years' worth of *True Confessions*. That's——"

Whatever else he might have said was lost in space. Like a mirage, *she* emerged from the landscape at that moment. Lips vaguely parted, showing just a gleam of a smile, her stride smooth and long. Six weeks after I'd first laid eyes on her, The Fantasy Jogger was there, looking more perfect than I'd ever imagined.

"Hi," she said, running by.

Then there was silence, and the momentary sense that all the air had been sucked out of my stomach.

"One of your friends?" Laura asked.

"I wish!"

"No doubt, she was saying hello to me," Big Walter suggested. "As you know, I have a way with women in the park."

"Not this time," Laura said, watching as The Fantasy Jogger moved ever more distant. "I think it was Tom . . . and I'm impressed."

An hour later, after saying good-bye to Laura, Big Walter and I went back to his apartment. Patricia was in the living room, looking absolutely ecstatic.

"There was a call for you," she announced, throwing her arms around Big Walter.

"Who was it?"

"A producer at Warner Brothers named Monte Robbins. He wants to talk to you about your screenplay tonight."

9

"BEING A BUILDING superintendent isn't a bad job," Big Walter once said. "I just happen to hate it."

Given the equanimity of his nature, it's hard to imagine Big Walter "hating" anything, but I understood what he meant. Mopping floors and picking up garbage were daily reminders that he wasn't making it at writing. Now, Big Walter stood face-to-face with the biggest opportunity of his life. Or, as Patricia stated after his telephone conversation with Monte Robbins, "We're on the verge of the greatest victory for the downtrodden since King John signed the Magna Carta."

Monte Robbins was an independent producer with an office on the Warner Brothers lot. That meant he could develop projects as he saw fit. If the studio liked what he did, it put up the money necessary to make the movie and assumed full rights. If not, Robbins was free to shop around somewhere else.

In truth, Robbins had the reputation of being something of a bastard. Thrice divorced, he'd had bitter splits with each of his wives, and wife number three became famous in her own right after the marriage ended by authoring a biography of her ex-husband entitled *Spoiled Rotten*. Among the revelations contained therein was the fact that their prenuptial agreement (later upheld by the California courts) cut her off without a penny in the event of divorce and gave Robbins the right to sleep around during the marriage with anyone he wanted. The book also recounted an incident when Robbins introduced his then-wife to a business associate with the words: "She has small tits, but makes up for it with her personality."

Like most producers, Robbins rarely invested his own cash, preferring to spend someone else's dollars instead. On more than one occasion, it was said that his generosity (such as it was) was "cost efficient," and *The National Enquirer* once published a copy of his federal income-tax return showing that, with a gross income of $4,000,000, Robbins had given $35 to charity. Still, Monte Robbins's reputation was excellent in one respect: he made movies, and his movies made money. No one knows exactly what makes a movie a hit. It's not the star. Dustin Hoffman made *Straight Time* and *Agatha* about the same time he was in *Kramer v. Kramer*, and the first two bombed completely. Nor is it a great screenplay. *Porky's*—which had no screenplay so to speak—grossed $100,000,000. Rather, hit movies result from a combination of intangibles, and Monte Robbins was a man with the Midas touch. After thirty years in the business, he had two dozen money-making films to his credit.

The screenplay that piqued Robbins's interest was Big Walter's buried-treasure epic. The plot revolved around lost

Incan gold worth hundreds of millions of dollars. Half a millennium ago, according to legend, the Incas had hidden their religious artifacts for safekeeping against the invading Spanish. Over time, the storage city was destroyed, but the treasure, hidden underground, remained intact. Now, high in the Andes Mountains, an Indiana Jones–type hero was on the verge of discovering the fortune. But villainous Nazi sympathizers were also closing in on the hoard.

Robbins liked the script—with reservations. "I'm not sure the site works," he told Big Walter. "South America doesn't interest American audiences, and you need a few more scenes with blood and violence. What I'd like is for you to do a rewrite. Change the locale from Peru to Egypt; make it a Tutankhamen-type treasure. Then get back to me, and we'll work a deal out."

"What kind of a deal?"

"Big bucks," Robbins answered. "I'm thinking feature film with someone like Clint Eastwood, but I'll need a rewrite by the end of the month. Can you do it?"

For a feature film with Clint Eastwood, Big Walter would have performed unnatural acts with a married Republican. "You'll have it," he promised.

Thus began what Big Walter called the most intense working period of his life. For the first time ever, he tasted success and it spurred him to new heights. Every morning, he was up at 6:00, writing until noon, when necessity demanded that he spend an hour or two on building work. Then he went back to his desk and typed until midnight, with an hour off for dinner. "I've never worked this hard on anything," he told me one night. "Everything I know about screenwriting is in this effort. But my ship's coming in. I can feel it."

Meanwhile, as August turned sticky and hot, my own efforts continued on *The Mariah Project*. In years past, I'd taken the month off; but, having decided to forgo a vacation until the book was finished, I spent most of my time in the Fordham library. Once or twice I suffered from "writer's block"—that strange malady which has afflicted writers from time immemorial—but each time I was able to overcome it. Writer's block, I concluded eventually, can be ascribed to three phenomena: (1) lack of discipline, (2) intellectual laziness, and (3) trying to write a scene that doesn't belong in a book.

Laura and I spent an increasing amount of time together, sometimes alone, sometimes with Big Walter. Usually we took walks or met for lunch. Once we went to an old Alfred Hitchcock movie. One of the things I liked most about her was her reliability. She never broke a date. She always returned telephone calls and did what she said she would. Occasionally, I felt sorry for Allen; at this point, I seemed to have a better relationship with his wife than he did. But since Laura and I weren't sleeping together, I considered myself absolved of all guilt.

As for The Fantasy Jogger, frustration ran rampant. No matter where or when I jogged, I didn't see her. An "irregular regular," she'd called herself. She ran "two or three times a week." But where?

"How should I know?" Big Walter answered one afternoon when I raised the subject. "Maybe she comes down to New York once every two months from Boston to visit her boyfriend. Have you ever thought of that?"

I hadn't—and the thought wasn't pleasant. The Fantasy Jogger, aka Carolyn Hewitt, had become quite real to me. "You have to understand," I said one afternoon, trying to explain myself to Patricia. "Writing a book is an incredible experience. It involves creating an entire world out of whole cloth and making it *real*. But this woman isn't just paper and ink. I've seen her. She's alive."

Thus, my enchantment continued as *The Mariah Project* developed. Hot on the trail of Ernest Reid, the murderous Kaleel Rashad moved north through India, leaving a trail of bodies behind. At the same time, the political arm of the PLO began putting pressure on its Washington contacts to learn the identity of CIA and Israeli agents assigned to the case. By late August, I'd written well over a hundred pages and developed a series of fail-safe writing habits. Then something happened which altered my working life: classes resumed at Fordham.

First-year law students are an odd lot. Most of them went through college as superachievers. By and large, they're aggressive and extremely tense. All of them are worried about grades, and most have difficulty coping with the case-study method that law-school professors love so much. Suddenly my sanctuary at the Fordham Law Library was overrun by three hundred traumatized twenty-one-year-olds, plus an even greater number of second- and third-year students. Desk space became a valuable commodity, and the library noise level increased markedly. However, one positive development did result. Quite quickly, the students became familiar faces. And, for the first time since leaving Columbia, I had what might be called an office social life.

Let me explain. Most people work at jobs where they're in constant communication with one another. Teachers have students and fellow faculty members. Shopkeepers deal with customers. Secretaries have their bosses and other office personnel to talk with. It's nice to take a break or just look around for twenty seconds and smile at someone else. Now, for the first time as a writer, I had that. Most of the students didn't know who I was, but just having familiar faces and eye contact was pleasant, and some of the women, in particular, seemed quite nice. As a professor at Columbia, I'd followed a self-imposed rule against dating students. But at

Fordham it occurred to me that, should the opportunity arise, there was no need for similar restraint.

Big Walter finished revising his screenplay just after Labor Day, marking the end of a herculean effort. He even gutted two previous screenplays, incorporating dialogue and a key plot twist from each in his buried-treasure epic. "It's the best thing I've ever written," he said.

I read it—and he was right.

Then, at a cost of $200, he had it typed professionally and Express Mailed to Warner Brothers.

"How long do you think it will take Monte Robbins to read it?" Patricia asked.

"Not too long," he told her. "Two or three weeks."

With the rewrite finished, both Walkers were able to slow down a little and relax. Patricia took a few days off, and they spent a long weekend together in upstate New York. Then Big Walter returned to the superintendent's duties he'd let slide the previous month, and, once again, we resumed jogging together. "Do you know how much Mallomars cost?" he asked one afternoon when we were running in the park.

"Not really."

"A dollar forty-nine a box. That's how much." Shaking his head, he continued to lumber at a slow, steady pace. "I always thought Mallomars were free. My mother never charged me for Mallomars when I was a kid."

"Don't worry about it," I comforted him. "When the money from Warner Brothers comes in, you'll be eating Mallomars with caviar on top."

That night, as I'd begun to do with increasing frequency, I spent the evening working on my book. For quite some time, David Barrett and Carolyn Hewitt had been lovers, but I'd never shown it. Now, in a town called Udaipur in central India, the air was fresh and warm. Sitting at the bedroom desk, I imagined a starlit sky over the Lake Palace Hotel, where hero and heroine were sheltered for the night. It was a scene I'd looked forward to writing for weeks. Take it slowly! Describe the setting. Moonbeams on water; ivory latticework against the nighttime sky; a castle built centuries ago by the Maharajah of Udaipur. It wasn't enough just to say how wonderful and warm Carolyn Hewitt was. I had to show it, describing her face, her mouth, her arms:

> Barrett lay beside her, envisioning a fire that consumed him entirely. Nothing else mattered. Nothing in the world existed except this woman and the ties that bound them together.

I wrote until dawn. Then, imagining she was still beside me, I went to sleep. Eight hours later, by the cold light of day, I sat in the Fordham library and reviewed what I had done. Change a word here, a sentence there. The scene worked.

Cheered, I looked around for someone to share the moment. The students were all sitting with faces buried in heavy legal texts. The library seemed cold and sterile. Somewhat disheartened, I got up and trudged downstairs to the basement cafeteria, where a half-dozen round tables stood evenly spaced. At one end of the cafeteria, a stainless steel serving counter fronted a collection of cellophane-wrapped pastries, sandwiches, and soggy meatloaf. A woman student, clad in a print blouse and jeans, crossed the room and took a seat alone at a corner table. Anxious for someone to talk with, I bought a cup of coffee and followed.

"Can I join you?"

"It's a free country," she said, giving me a look that felt like being doused with cold water.

Normally, I'd have walked off, but, at that particular moment, any companionship seemed better than none. The table was covered with paper cups, napkins, and empty soda cans from earlier residents.

"Did you drink all those yourself?" I asked, pointing toward the litter.

Ms. Charm half-smiled.

"My name is Tom Hammond. I'm a professor-turned-writer."

"So how come you're in the law-school cafeteria?"

Slowly but surely, a conversation developed. Ms. Charm turned out to be named Sylvia Pennock—a second-year law student from Glenn Falls, Idaho. "Have you heard of Glenn Falls?" she inquired.

"No, but I've heard of Idaho."

While somewhat guarded, she was quite bright, and, at times, hinted at being nice. We talked for about twenty minutes, dividing our time between *The Mariah Project* and the Federal Equal Employment Opportunity Act. Halfway through the conversation, we were joined by a friend of Sylvia's named Kathy Hart. Ms. Hart was polite, but seemed more annoyed than pleased by my presence, so I excused myself and went back upstairs to write. Soon after, the ball-point pen I was using ran out of ink, which I took as a sign from the gods that I should quit work for the rest of the day and go jogging with Big Walter. Once upon a time, a feeling of guilt would have attended such slothfulness, but Big Walter had a way of putting things in perspective. "Never feel guilty about screwing off," he counseled when I showed up at his apartment. "You're not wasting time, you're enjoying it."

Our run was uneventful, save for a wild daisy I found growing in the park.

"She loves me; she loves me not. She loves me; she loves me not." One by one, I pulled off the petals. *"She loves me!"* The verdict was in! The Fantasy Jogger and I were in love! Thankful for small favors, I put the deciding petal in my pocket for luck.

That night, I went back to my book. Kaleel Rashad arrived in Udaipur with a team of assassins. David Barrett and Carolyn Hewitt narrowly escaped death on the lake. Laura called just before midnight, but I was too busy to talk.

"I'm right in the middle of an important passage," I told her. "Could we talk tomorrow?"

"I guess so. Are you free for lunch?"

Something in her voice suggested jealousy. This was the first time I'd been the one to end a conversation between us. Normally it was Laura who had someplace to go or something to do; but, at the moment, I was anxious to return to Udaipur and Carolyn Hewitt.

"Lunch is good," I answered. "You pick a place."

The following afternoon, we met at Tavern on the Green in Central Park. The food was fair, the service mediocre.

"Maybe it's the waiter's break," Laura posited as we waited thirty minutes for menus and the chance to order.

"More likely, it's his day off."

Afterward, we took a walk through Central Park. The late September leaves had begun to fall. The sky was cloudless.

"I made the bulletin board at NBC," Laura said, brushing a strand of hair from her cheek. "Some asshole stuck a note with my name on it next to the camera assignments."

"What did it say?"

"I suppose it could be taken as a compliment. The gist of the message was that there are certain parts of my anatomy that the author admires and wants to fondle, although he didn't use quite that language."

"How do you know it was a he?"

"Women have better taste than that."

Weighing my options, I decided not to contest the issue. "What else is new at the office?"

"Not much," she said. "The Seven O'clock News went down a point in the Nielsen ratings, but Tom Brokaw is away on vacation, so it doesn't count. Johnny Carson extended his contract, which makes a lot of people happy. That's about it."

"What about the marital front?"

"Things are pretty much what you'd expect. Allen keeps saying he doesn't want to upset the applecart, and I keep telling him that the apples fell off our cart a long time ago. Each week, I check the *New York Times* apartment listings, but there's never anything near the office for less than fourteen hundred a month."

"Why don't you ask Roger Mudd to lead off the evening news with a request for an apartment?"

"Right—or maybe Allen could drop dead." A pained look crossed her face as the words escaped. "I didn't mean that. Really, I didn't. It's just, you need a certain amount of anger to separate."

We walked in silence; not touching, but still somehow able to communicate. So much about Laura—her face, her walk, the way she held her body—spoke.

"These must be strange times for you," I said finally.

"All times are strange."

"Would you rather not talk about it?"

"To the contrary, you're the only person I feel comfortable talking with. Most of my friends know Allen, and their loyalty is split. You're the only person I can count on for support."

"I'm flattered."

"I hope so. Incidentally, I meant to tell you, my parents were in town last week, and we had dinner with Augustus."

"And?"

"It was very nice. Allen was in Chicago on business, and Augustus went out of his way to be charming. He's quite a gourmet. Dinner was spectacular, and he cooked it himself in the famous garden behind his town house.''

"Did my name come up?"

"Only once. I mentioned you in passing, but my parents were there, so I couldn't say too much."

The sun had started its downward slide, indicating it was nearly 4:00. It was the first time I could recall being with Laura that she hadn't looked at her watch.

"Tom, where do we stand in this relationship?"

The question caught me off guard completely.

"I'm not sure," I said, groping for a response. "I guess, up until now, you've pretty much dictated the pace."

"Have I?"

"Yes."

Just for a moment, I could hear Allen mocking, "Sounds familiar; that's the way she is with me, too."

A little disordered, I waited for a hint of what was next.

"Tomorrow is my birthday," Laura said. "I'll be thirty-one years old. There's a present I want."

"Something from Saks?"

"Not quite." The self-effacing smile I'd seen before was back. "Tom, I've thought this over pretty carefully. I want you to be my lover."

10

S O WE BECAME lovers, and the friendship remained. Laura telephoned almost every night. Our daytime rendezvous grew more frequent. Looking back, I won't make a value judgment on the propriety of having an affair with a married woman—or vice versa. I'll simply say it happened because both of us wanted it to happen.

Laura's hours at NBC—she was still working the midnight to 8:00 A.M. shift—made getting together during the afternoon a relatively easy matter. Sometimes she'd come over to the Fordham Law Library to keep me company while I wrote. Once we rented a car and spent the day in Sleepy Hollow, trudging through fallen autumn leaves that had to be kicked aside to find a path. Several days later, coincidental with Rosh Hashanah, we had lunch with Big Walter and Patricia at a Mexican restaurant on Columbus Avenue—our "coming-out party," so to speak.

"I love Rosh Hashanah," Big Walter announced midway through his second margarita.

"Why?"

"Because alternate-side-of-the-street parking is suspended."

"I didn't know we owned a car," Patricia interrupted.

"We don't. But think of all the other people it makes happy."

After lunch, we went to the Metropolitan Museum of Art and spent several hours with Rembrandt and Botticelli. "When it comes to friends," Laura told me at day's end, "you have good taste."

Like much of our time together, the afternoon drew us closer. Still, we led very separate lives. Laura's home telephone was off-limits. Allen seemed less real to me than imagined. I still wasn't sure what went on inside Laura's head. And there was no way I could confide in her about The Fantasy Jogger.

"Maybe I'm psychotic," I said one night, talking with Big Walter. "My love life consists of a woman who's married to someone else and a quasi-fictitious literary character."

"Which one is more important to you?"

"I'm not sure," I admitted.

"Do you want my opinion?"

"Judging by the look on your face, probably not."

"I'll tell you anyway," he said. "Any day now, I expect you to fall in love with a department-store mannequin."

The point was well taken, but the reality of my life remained unchanged. Every time I went jogging, I looked for The Fantasy Jogger. And every time I didn't see her, I returned home disappointed.

October passed without word from Monte Robbins. Fearful that the United States Postal Service had somehow fouled up, Big Walter telephoned Warner Brothers to find out whether the screenplay had been delivered. "It's here," a secretary reported, "but Mr. Robbins has been quite busy lately. He'll get back to you once he's read it."

"Maybe you're using the wrong approach," Patricia suggested when the conversation ended and Big Walter had hung up. "Tell Robbins you're six foot three, weigh two hundred seventy pounds, and are getting pissed."

That night, growing ever more anxious, Big Walter penned a short note:

Dear Mr. Robbins,

Eight weeks have passed since I sent you the revised version of *Treasure*. The project is extremely important to me, and I'd appreciate some word on its progress.

Sincerely,
Walter Walker

There was no response.

"Sure, I'm nervous," Big Walter admitted to me over dinner one night. "I've spent my entire adult life waiting for an opportunity like this. Every morning, I ask myself how much longer I'll have to wait. But they're going to make the movie. I know it."

Meanwhile, *The Mariah Project* continued on schedule. The trail of Ernest Reid led north through India, then toward the Middle East—home ground for Kaleel Rashad; dangerous terrain for David Barrett and Carolyn Hewitt. A double agent was uncovered at Israeli Intelligence headquarters in Jerusalem. Once again, hero and heroine narrowly escaped death—this time in Pakistan. By mid-November, I was well past the two-hundred-page mark and going strong. The book had everything: good pacing, a strong plot, characters who mattered.

As for my "office" at Fordham, things continued on an

even keel. I met a few more students, learned which pay telephones returned quarters, and grew friendlier with Sylvia Pennock. In some ways, she was a little distant—my standing offer for lunch was met with a standing rejection. But she was unfailingly pleasant and good company for coffee in the school cafeteria. Also, although I hadn't focused on it the day we met, Sylvia was quite attractive: medium height, long black hair, a very pretty face, and exceptionally good figure. Ill-fitting clothes had obscured the latter asset the day we met; but, as her wardrobe varied, it revealed ample curves in all the right places. I appreciated Sylvia most one afternoon when we were working at the same library table. Nearby, a pair of first-year students were talking incessantly, making it virtually impossible for me to concentrate. Finally I asked for quiet, and one of them answered, "You don't go to school here. You can't tell us to be quiet."

"Hey, shithead!" Sylvia snapped, looking up from her book. "Shut the fuck up."

(For the record, I should note that Sylvia's friend, Kathy Hart, rarely said hello, and the only conversation I can recall having with her took place one afternoon in the library when she came over and asked, "Where's Sylvia?")

Thanksgiving came and went. The weather turned cold, which cut down on my jogging. Laura continued her hunt for an apartment. Patricia and I went down to watch the tree-lighting ceremony at Rockefeller Center. Boosted by a series of late-night writing sessions, *The Mariah Project* neared three hundred pages. *The New York Times Magazine* ran an article titled: "Augustus Hasson—Publishing's Superstar."

"In the world of blockbuster books," the article began, "the mention of Augustus Hasson induces a Pavlovian response: publishers, writers and producers all salivate." Then in somewhat less hyperbolic fashion, the piece recounted a

typical Hasson day: working hours—8:00 A.M. to 8:00 P.M.;
number of letters dictated—thirty; time spent on the telephone—
three hours; meetings; negotiations; work ad infinitum.

"I never use outside readers," The Great One was quoted
as saying. "I review all manuscripts and proposals myself.
Indeed, I find it quite difficult to delegate any authority to
subordinates." Midway through the article, the famous garden lunches were discussed: "In addition to his literary tal-
ents, Hasson is an uncompromising gourmet. When a recent
meal concluded with chocolate mousse, the agent instructed
his maid to beat the whipped cream until just before it was
ready. Hasson himself then added the finishing touches to
make certain the consistency was just right."

There was Augustus Hasson on would-be clients: "I get
scores of unsolicited manuscripts in the mail each week, and
an astonishingly high percentage are awful." Augustus Hasson
on his reputation for arriving late at formal dinners: "Like
Louis the Fourteenth, I'm always on time; everyone else is
early." And Augustus Hasson on the publishing industry
vis-à-vis his own success: "I realized long ago that I could
exploit the system far more easily than I could change it."

"Can I say something?" Big Walter queried after I showed
him the article.

"Go ahead."

"I'm glad he's your agent and all that. But, once *The
Mariah Project* is sold to a publisher, I think civilization
would be well served if Augustus Hasson were run over by a
truck."

A few days later, Laura expressed a contrary view. "I
know Augustus's ego is a bit much," she said. "But give
him credit. Success didn't come on a silver platter. He earned
it."

As she made the remark, we were lying naked on the bed
in my apartment—one of many such encounters since the

resumption of sexual relations between us. Laura was on her back with a sheet pulled up to her waist, well below the curve of her breasts. An hour earlier we'd made love, and now the conversation meandered wherever our minds led it.

"You know something," she said, running a finger across my chest. "For someone who drives himself professionally as hard as you do, you're surprisingly mellow." Sitting up, she grabbed a pillow and brought it down hard on top of my head. "But that doesn't excuse jumping out of bed in the middle of making love to write something down on a piece of lined yellow paper."

"Ow! Ouch!"

Again the pillow struck.

"Listen! Ouch! Writers are eccentric. Shakespeare used to jump out of bed all the time after making love."

"Maybe *after,* but never in the middle, like he was writing down the minutes of a meeting——pervert!"

"Don't call me a pervert. You're the one who—— Ouch!"

"Come on, Hammond. Be tough! Grab a pillow and defend yourself!"

The assault continued until I retaliated in kind, seizing a pillow and wielding it like a medieval ax. Then the tide turned, after which the struggle ceased and we lay side-by-side, quiet. For a moment, there was silence. Laura moved closer, resting her head on my chest.

"You're quite something," she said. "Do you know that?"

I waited, curious as to what was coming next.

"Why haven't you ever been married?"

"I don't know," I answered, marveling at her gift for the unexpected. "I guess, for a long time I wasn't ready. Then, around the time I turned thirty, I got involved with a woman who was right in some ways and wrong in others."

"So you left?"

"Yes."

Drawing her hand back, she looked toward me. "That's the way it is with most relationships. Men tend to leave first. No matter how bad things are, women are reluctant to give up."

"Do you really believe that?"

"Tom, there's something I should tell you. . . . Allen and I went to bed together the other night."

I lay still, not knowing what to expect next.

"Don't just lie there," Laura pleaded. "Say something."

"Like what?"

"I don't know. Ask me how it was. Tell me I'm stupid. But say something."

"All right. How was it?"

The corners of her mouth turned up. "You know something? You're whacko. No one else would put up with me the way you do."

"What can I say? I like you."

Just for a moment, I saw a look—as though, for the first time, she understood. Reaching out, she took my hand and touched each finger to her lips.

"Are you angry . . . about Allen?"

"A little."

"Don't be," she said. "It was a mistake. . . . For months, I've slept in a different bed. He hasn't held me, or kissed me. I won't even let him in the same room when I'm naked. Last week I started to feel sorry—for both of us. So, when Allen told me he wanted to make love more than anything he'd ever wanted in his life, I said yes."

"And?"

"It was awful. When we kissed, I was the one to move my lips away first. When he touched my breasts, I felt dirty. For a while, I wasn't sure he'd be able to consummate. And, when it was over, he lay beside me and cried. Right now, there's nothing more to say, except it was the most painful experience of my life. And I thought you should know about it."

Big Walter was in the boiler room, working to restore hot water for the building, when I went over that night. For whatever reason, he was unusually subdued and quiet.

"What's the matter?"

"Nothing," he said. "It's just, sometimes I get a little sick of mopping floors and cleaning up garbage; of dealing with people who make a lot of money so they don't bother to say things like 'please,' 'excuse me,' 'hello,' or 'thank you.' " Leaning forward, he gave the pop valve a sharp twist, and a thin wisp of steam escaped the boiler. "That should do it. How's Laura?"

"Fine. What about Patricia?"

"Just great, considering she's married to a building superintendent."

Waiting in silence, I digested the comment. Big Walter gathered his tools and began walking toward the basement stairs.

"Sometimes I think that writing *Kansas Sunset* was the worst thing that ever happened to me," he said as I followed. "If it wasn't for that poem, maybe now I'd have a decent job."

"Okay, big fellow. What's the matter? Out with it."

Taking his keys from a back pocket, Big Walter opened the door to his apartment and stepped inside. Patricia was by the sofa.

"Did you tell him?"

"Not yet," Big Walter answered.

Moving close, she embraced her husband and gave him a kiss. "Just remember, behind those clouds, there's a sun shining. Nobody's perfect, but I love you. You're one hundred percent right for me."

Face up on the coffee table was a letter with the Warner Brothers logo on top:

Dear Mr. Walker,

Thank you for letting me see *Treasure*. Unfortunately, it's not suited to our needs.

Sincerely,
Monte Robbins

11

DECEMBER BROUGHT THE holiday season into view, but otherwise my life remained unchanged. Laura and I continued our personalized brand of friendship. Big Walter picked himself up and began work on a new screenplay. "I read something once," he told me the day after he began anew. "Screenwriting is like running alongside a giant boulder that's rolling downhill. At the same time you're trying to guide its course, you have to be careful not to get crushed."

Meanwhile, *The Mariah Project* moved on inexorably. Energized by my work, I spent day after day in the Fordham library; writing, crossing out, polishing my creation. Carolyn Hewitt remained ideal. More than ever, she and The Fantasy Jogger blended as one. And, despite Laura, I often found myself slipping into fantasy as a means of gratification.

Kaleel Rashad finally caught up with Ernest Reid in Ankara. Hours later, when David Barrett and Carolyn Hewitt arrived, they discovered the scientist's corpse hanging in a makeshift torture chamber. The degree of mutilation made it likely that Reid had resisted revealing some piece of information to his captors, and that meant evidence of the crystals' location might still be found. Sifting through Reid's papers and piecing together what was already known, hero and heroine reconstructed the dead man's movements over the past forty-eight hours. Maybe—just maybe—Reid had shared his secret in the hope of preserving the crystals' find. A book of matches bearing the insignia of a Turkish merchant was their only clue.

The merchant knew nothing of the crystals, but he did remember "a very nervous, very frightened man." Reid had come seeking a hiding place for a map of the ocean floor. A bank safe-deposit box was "out of the question," the scientist had said. It would be too easy for his pursuers to find. Not wanting to become involved, the merchant had turned Reid's pleas aside. Nothing else was worthy of mention— except for one item. The merchant remembered Reid saying that even a bank would be preferable to . . . the merchant strained, trying to recall. "I am embarrassed for the lady," he said at last, bowing toward Carolyn Hewitt. "But I believe the document he sought to protect was hidden in a brothel."

Looking up from the index cards and yellow paper spread over the library table in front of me, I saw Big Walter gazing down.

"Good to see you," he announced, his face beaming.

"What in God's name are you doing here?"

"Just curious to see your office; that's all." Several tables away, Sylvia Pennock and Kathy Hart were engrossed in a study of legal periodicals. At the sound of voices, Kathy issued a sharp *sshh*.

"She's kind of cute," Big Walter whispered, casting a sideways glance.

"Look, Big Walter. I work here, and I don't have a student ID card. Don't get me kicked out."

"Perish the thought. I just came to visit. How about that one over there—the one with the red hair and big——"

"Out! Before I do something drastic!"

Majestically, Big Walter sniffled, assuming his most hurt little-boy look. "All right. I'll leave if you want."

"Don't take it personally. If you promise never to come back, I'll buy you a popsicle."

The bargain struck, I gathered my notes and started toward the library exit. Big Walter followed, pulling even as we reached the lobby.

"There's something I want to ask you," he said.

"What is it?"

"Could you tell me where the ladies' room is?"

"The what!"

"The ladies' room. I'm working on a screenplay, and there's a scene where one of the characters goes into a ladies' room. I need to do some firsthand research."

Shaking my head, I pointed across the lobby to a steel-grey door next to the security guard's desk. "Be my guest. Do you want me to call Patricia now or after you're arrested?"

"Neither. We can come back tonight at midnight after the library closes."

"Big Walter, what exactly do you mean by *we*?"

"You and me, of course. You don't expect me to do this alone, do you?"

Let me explain as best I can why I wound up in the vicinity of the Fordham Law School ladies' room that midnight. Number one: I'm crazy. That was the primary motivating factor. Number two: Big Walter (who, after all, is my best friend) asked me to help. And number three: I was curious to see just how far he'd carry what I assumed was a bluff. Regardless, at 12:01 A.M., we entered the law-school building together and approached the guard on duty at the security desk. The lobby was dark. Up ahead, I saw the glass library doors and, behind them, a lone woman student working late beneath a solitary row of lights.

"You're crazy!" I muttered under my breath. "Any normal person would ask Patricia to go in during the day to see what the ladies' room looks like."

"I told you," Big Walter whispered. "I did ask, and she wouldn't do it."

The guard motioned for us to stop.

"Excuse me," I said, gathering my courage. "My wallet's missing, and I think it fell out somewhere in the stacks. Would it be all right if I went in to take a look?"

Suspiciously, he eyed us both. "What makes you think you gonna find sumpthin' in the dark?"

"I don't know. Maybe I could borrow your flashlight."

"It's real important," Big Walter added. "His baby's picture is in the wallet. Why don't you go keep an eye on him, and I'll stand guard here at the desk until you get back."

Weighing his options, the guard seemed torn between humanitarian concern, devotion to duty, and an inclination to sit on his butt. "All right," he said at last, looking toward Big Walter. "Anyone comes in, you stop 'em, till I finish taking a look."

Except for the aforementioned woman student, the library was empty. The heat was shut off, so it was pretty cold, and the stacks were dark.

"Over there," I said, pointing to a faraway spot. "There's where I did most of my work tonight."

Obediently, the guard scanned the floor with his flashlight.

"Ain't nothin' there."

"Maybe it's a little more toward the back."

"Don't see nuthin' there neither. You sure you lost it tonight?"

"Pretty sure, yes, sir."

The woman student stood up, and, leaving her books behind, walked toward the lobby.

"How about beneath that table over there?" I suggested.

Slowly, we moved toward the designated spot.

"Ain't nuthin'. You sure this is right?"

"Yes, sir. It should be here someplace unless——"

The woman returned, looking quite excited. "Excuse me," she called, rushing toward us. "There's a strange man in the ladies' room taking notes."

"Stay here!" I ordered, breaking into a run before the guard could react. "I'll check it out."

For the record, the ladies' room at the Fordham Law Library has three toilet stalls and three sinks. The walls are dressed in cream-colored squares, with gold tiles underfoot. For those truly interested, I should add reference to a mirror, a paper-towel machine, and a Tampax dispenser in the corner. Big Walter was standing by the mirror, true to the lady's word, taking notes.

"Okay, big fellow. Out!"

"Just a minute. I'm almost finished."

"We're *both* almost finished. Hurry up!"

Untroubled by the moment, Big Walter's face assumed a questioning look. "What do you suppose that shelf beneath the mirror is for?"

"Combs and makeup. Jesus Christ! Will you hurry up!"

"Don't get excited. I'm coming."

"So's Christmas. Get a move on it."

Smiling benignly, Big Walter folded his pad and stuffed it

in a back pocket. I waited, anticipating the wail of police sirens at any moment.

"Earth to Big Walter! Earth to Big Walter! Will you *please* hurry up!"

"All right," he said. "I'm ready; and thank you very much."

"You're welcome. All I can say is, your screenplay better be very good."

"What screenplay?"

Speechless, I stared at my cohort. "Big Walter, what did you mean by that last comment?"

"Nothing much."

"Big Walter, I'm going to ask you something, and I want an honest answer. Is there or is there not a screenplay in progress?"

"Of course not!"

"Then why?"

Looking happier than I've ever seen him, Big Walter shrugged. "Actually, it's a practical joke. But, before you kill me, be honest! When was the last time you had as much fun as you've had tonight?"

Remarkably, we escaped. And, more remarkably, no repercussions followed—although, when we told Patricia about it, she said that someday soon she was going to give Big Walter a gift certificate for a psychiatrist. The next morning, I was back at my desk in the library working on *The Mariah Project*. Thereafter, December continued on course. Laura began making plans to go to the Caribbean—alone—over Christmas and New Year's. Big Walter bought a small evergreen tree and dressed it with holiday ornaments for the building lobby. After modest reflection, I decided to send a Christmas card to Augustus Hasson, then regretted my choice when I returned home one afternoon to find a *New York Post* gossip item slipped under my door by Big Walter. In relevant part, the article read:

> The most exclusive annual literary gathering in New York took place yesterday at the East Side town house of superagent Augustus Hasson. Hasson, whose clients have sold an estimated 800 million books, throws a Christmas party each year to introduce his clients to a select group of editors, screen stars, and movie moguls. Among those in attendance were Warren Beatty, Francis Ford Coppola, Farrah Fawcett—and, of course, Hasson's star-studded author list.

"Just wait!" read Big Walter's scrawl across the article's face. "Someday, we'll give a party for Paul Newman and Robert Redford. And, when we do, Augustus Hasson won't be invited."

For several days, I pondered the implications inherent in being left off The Great One's Christmas list. Then I decided it didn't matter. What counted was his interest in me *after* he read *The Mariah Project*, and, with that in mind, I pushed harder. My writing day stretched longer. The book grew better. Four days before Christmas, I interrupted my work for a *bon voyage* dinner with Laura at an Indian restaurant on Amsterdam Avenue. Because of her work schedule, we dined at 6:00, then went back to my apartment.

"You know something," I said when our coats were off and we'd settled on the sofa. "I'm sorry I won't be with you for Christmas."

For most of the evening, her mood had been quiet. Now without changing expression, she leaned back, eyes half-shut. "Christmas is for children," she said. "Children and happy lovers. Everyone else just goes through the motions."

"Do you really believe that?"

"Yes. And so do you." Straightening up, she looked toward me. "There was a time when I thought our generation might have a new set of answers; but the truth is, love and family are still what life is all about. That's what's so hard about leaving Allen. I might not find a new life with anyone else."

"You can't mean that."

"Yes, I do. Sometimes I think I've grown too cynical and too old to fall in love." Ruefully, she smiled. "I guess that's not very optimistic, is it? But being alone eight hundred miles from home won't be the best way to spend Christmas."

I waited for whatever else lay ahead.

"Christmas used to be a good day for us," she said, continuing the thought. "So was New Year's. We'd dress up, get drunk, cook dinner, and go to bed. This year, I told Allen to get a date so he wouldn't be alone, which was one of the more insensitive things I've ever said." The smile was gone. "I guess that's in keeping with the rest of me. Right now, I can't seem to do anything right."

"Don't get down on yourself. The waters might seem turbulent now, but the ship is sound. You'll make it through all right."

"Maybe, maybe not."

"How long are you going to let Allen's weakness dictate your life?"

There was no response, and I was aware of a slight hardening creeping into my voice.

"Laura, I'm trying to help, but not everything you do seems constructive. We've known each other for seven months. You told me you were leaving your husband the day we met. This started in May; now it's December. There's snow on the ground——"

"That's enough," she said.

"Is it?"

"Look, Tom; don't play a power game with me. You don't own me. And until you've gone through what I'm going through, maybe you should just keep quiet."

"Don't you understand?" I prodded. "You have to get on with the rest of your life."

"And what about Allen? What's he supposed to do with the rest of his?" Hands trembling, she opened her purse and thrust out an ivory card that lay folded on top. "Here! This came with a gold bracelet I found on my pillow last night. Read it!"

Dear Laura,——

> I love you, and always will.
> With you, my life fits together.
> Without you, there are just broken
> pieces.

> Forever,
> *Allen*

"So do me a favor; no more lectures—about Allen or anything else. I know you care about me. But so does my husband."

Christmas came and went. The Fordham Law Library shut down for intersession, and the National Football League playoffs began. Big Walter spent the better part of two days repairing the building boiler, which broke twice. Toward the end of December, Patricia called to invite me for New Year's Eve dinner.

"Are you sure I won't be in the way?" I asked.

"Don't be silly. What could be better than being kissed by two glamorous men at midnight?"

"Being kissed by one glamorous woman," I told her.

The last outstanding copy of Big Walter's screenplay came back with a rejection letter. A "wish-you-were-here" card postmarked the Virgin Islands arrived from Laura. "Sprinkle some sand in your bed tonight?" she suggested. "Then you can pretend you're here on vacation in the Caribbean."

On December 31, taking advantage of a break in the cold, I went for a midafternoon run in Riverside Park. The promenade was deserted, the splintered wood benches bare. A stiff wind picked up as I began to run. What a year it had been: *The Mariah Project,* Laura, The Fantasy Jogger. All part of my life; all inchoate and unfulfilled. Up ahead, a solitary figure came into view. "You know what I'd really like to do tonight," I thought to myself. "I'd like to dress up, stay home, cook a wonderful dinner, and be with The Fantasy Jogger." The oncoming figure, a woman in her forties, drew closer. Lengthening my stride, I ran past her.

Fate! Destiny! That was how the world turned. Maybe The Fantasy Jogger would be up ahead, sitting on a bench, shivering and forlorn. And, when I appeared, her look would change to a warm welcoming smile. Poetic justice for all the times I'd lain awake wishing she were beside me . . . 91st Street . . . 100th . . . No one. The trees were bare; the wind was cold. She was a writer! The day I'd first seen her, The Fantasy Jogger had told me she was a writer. What better match could I hope for? Sensing the futility in going on, I turned toward home. Maybe next year would be different. After all, things worthwhile take time to nourish and grow. As for now, Big Walter and Patricia were good friends. New Year's Eve would be better spent with them than alone.

The Mariah Project moved on. David Barrett and Carolyn Hewitt found Ernest Reid's legacy in an Ankara brothel. For $50 American, the proprietor surrendered the map, not knowing he had bartered a piece of paper that could reshape the world. Shadowing their every move, Kaleel Rashad waited for the opportunity to kill. Unaware of the danger, hero and heroine continued on.

Laura returned from the Caribbean with a fabulous tan. Sylvia Pennock and I finally had lunch together in the school cafeteria. A monster snowstorm hit New York, dropping twelve inches of snow on the sidewalk in front of Big Walter's building.

"I know it snowed on the rest of Manhattan," Big Walter grumbled. "But this sidewalk is the only one I care about. You would, too, if you had to shovel it." Two hours after the task was done, a municipal snowplow went off at an angle and dumped three feet of snow back on the sacred spot that Big Walter had just shoveled. "Normally, I don't get mad," proclaimed Superintendent Walker. "But, at this particular moment, I'm enraged, furious, and totally incensed."

The next day it snowed again—so hard that I felt I was inside one of those toy globes you turn upside-down and watch as the snow cascades down on the figures within. Overcome by an attack of sympathy, I helped Big Walter shovel the sidewalk, after which we went to the park and made snow angels (they're harder than snowmen).

Patricia got another raise. Kathy Hart actually said hello to me in the Fordham library. Three weeks after Christmas, Big Walter got around to taking down the lobby Christmas tree after the tenants' committee overruled his contention that it "wasn't hurting anyone." *The Mariah Project* neared its inevitable end.

Kaleel Rashad approached David Barrett at a ticket counter in the Athens airport, thrust a revolver in Barrett's ribs, and ordered the American toward a side door. Catching sight of them just before they disappeared from view, Carolyn Hewitt followed. Gunfire! Chaos! When order was restored, Rashad lay dead. Carolyn Hewitt—lover, partner, companion, friend—

had become David Barrett's savior as well. But was the map accurate? Would the crystals be found?

Naskanik Archipelago—the South Pacific. Two days later. Depth sounders bounced acoustic signals off the ocean floor; divers submerged; computers whirred. Onboard ship, David Barrett and Carolyn Hewitt stood waiting. In Washington and Jerusalem, hearts pounded. The world balance of power was about to change. . . . *The crystals were there! The Mariah Project had come to an end.*

Gathering my papers, I looked around. It was a Tuesday night, well past 11:00. The Fordham library seemed cold and austere. *The book was done*—a moment to share. But with whom? Where? Cognizant of the hour, I eliminated potential celebrants one by one. Laura was at work, and would be until 8:00 A.M. Big Walter and Patricia went to bed at 11:00. On the balcony above, Sylvia Pennock sat engrossed in a copy of the Uniform Commercial Code. "Entirely appropriate," I decided. After all, Sylvia and I had shared the same office since August. Hoping for the best, I climbed the stairs.

"It's finished," I told her.

"What's finished?"

"The book. I thought maybe you'd like to have a drink to celebrate."

Considering the offer, Sylvia set her copy of the UCC aside. "Wait here. I'll be back in a minute." Put on hold, I watched as she crossed to a table where Kathy Hart sat studying alone. The two women conferred, and Sylvia began what appeared to be an exercise in persuasion. Finally, she returned. "Congratulations! Even Kathy admits it's exciting. Why don't you come over for a drink?"

"Over where?"

"Our apartment. Kathy and I are roommates. Don't worry, she won't bite."

*   *   *

Outside, a thin layer of frost glistened on the city streets. The air was cold; the night sky, cloudy. At a small brownstone on West 69th Street, Sylvia pointed to the stoop and we went inside, climbing the stairs to a fourth-floor apartment. The furniture was old, but well kept. Kathy took my coat and hung it on a rack near the door.

"This is home," Sylvia said. "What would you like to drink?"

"I don't know. Whatever you've got."

"I'll tell you what. As long as we're celebrating, let's do a couple of lines instead." Sitting on the sofa, she took a small glass vial from her breast pocket and tapped it gently. A half-gram of fine white powder fell to a brass plate beside her. Then, as I watched, she reached for a razor blade and began to cut, fashioning thin white lines two inches long. "That should do it. Have you ever tried coke?"

"Not really," I answered.

"You do it like this." Sticking the end of a tightly rolled dollar bill in her nostril, Sylvia inhaled, sliding her nose down the first white line. "Don't worry," she assured me. "Walt Disney did it all the time."

"I think I'll pass."

The dollar bill passed to Kathy, whose face was in profile, showing features that seemed much prettier now that I was taking the time to look.

"How do you feel?" Sylvia asked her.

"Kind of nice."

I began to relax. The room was quiet and dimly lit. Sylvia looked particularly sexy, dressed in jeans and a tight-fitting gold blouse.

"Should we tell him now?" Kathy prodded.

"Tell me what?"

Surreptitiously, the two women exchanged glances, then moved closer to one another.

"It's like this," Sylvia said. "Kathy and I are lovers. Haven't you figured out why we invited you back here yet?"

The morning sun was barely above the horizon when I stumbled back to my apartment. Dazed, I pondered the hours just passed, then changed into pajamas preparatory to bed. "Brush your teeth," I told myself. "Then check the telephone-answering machine and get some sleep."

"Hi! This is Laura," the first message said. "I found an apartment. Moving day is Sunday."

PART THREE

12

AS PLEDGED, LAURA moved on Sunday. Big Walter and I offered to help, but our services were declined on the theory that Allen didn't need to see his wife walking out the door with another man. Part of me was surprised that the move occurred at all. During the preceding months, I'd come to doubt Laura's resolve; so much so that, in some ways, I'd retreated emotionally from whatever it was we'd once shared. The question now was whether we could reach out and establish more in the way of confidence and trust in one another.

"I'd like you to come for dinner," she announced when I telephoned the day after the move to find out if everything was all right. "Right now, things are pretty hectic, but Saturday would be nice."

Pursuant to instructions, I arrived Saturday night at 8:00. Laura met me at the door to her apartment and led the way inside. The building was a modern high-rise, located several blocks east of Central Park. The apartment consisted of a living room, bedroom, and walk-in kitchen—all fully decorated. Considering the fact that Laura had moved in less than a week earlier, the transformation from empty rooms to a home was remarkable.

"The carpets are new," she told me as we moved through the living room to a large picture window overlooking the street. "So's the living-room furniture and bed. Everything else is from my prior residence." Next to the sofa, I stopped to admire a painting of birch trees in the snow. "That's a Nolte," Laura explained. "The most prolific painter who ever lived."

"Man or woman?"

"Woman. She was my great-aunt. For four decades, she honored my parents with the gift of a painting a week. Each one came with an ornate wood frame that made stacking impossible. By the time I was twenty, we had a thousand Noltes stuffed in drawers, falling out of closets, piled in the garage and basement. Once a year, she'd come to visit, and we'd run around like lunatics, hanging Noltes all over the place. When Allen and I got married, we needed some artwork for our apartment. My father's words, as I recall, were, 'Kids, take all the Noltes you want.' "

"It's kind of nice," I said, moving in for a closer look.

"That's why we took it. The other nine hundred ninety-nine aren't so hot." Repeating a gesture I'd seen often, Laura glanced at her watch. "Don't worry. I don't have another date. It's just I made lasagna this afternoon and put it in the oven twenty minutes ago. This is my first date in seven years, and I don't want to screw it up."

The lasagna was ready a half-hour later. Just before dinner, Laura dimmed the lights and put candles on the table, making the atmosphere decidedly romantic. For most of the meal, we conversed on safe subjects, neither of us venturing a jarring note.

"Did you really like the lasagna?" she asked when supper was finished.

"Absolutely! If I went to a restaurant and your lasagna was on the menu, I'd order it."

The look of relief etched on her face made it clear that making dinner was not an everyday Laura Kinney occurrence. Working in tandem, we washed the dishes, then went back to the living room and settled on the sofa. So far, everything had gone right, except neither of us had risked broaching the subject that was important. Finally, I broke the ice.

"What's it like to be thirty-one and single?"

Looking as though she had mixed feelings on the topic, Laura shrugged. "It's strange, it's wonderful, it's frustrating, it's nice. You name it and, over the past six days, I've felt it."

"What was it like moving out?"

"Awful. Seven years ago, the night before Allen and I got married, we stayed up till four in the morning drinking cognac. And I remember thinking then, 'Oh, my God! We've thrown out all our double copies of books and records. What happens to "Sergeant Pepper" and "Johnny's Greatest Hits" if we split?' Last Saturday, I found out. We spent twelve hours divvying up our lives and putting things in boxes. Half the day, I cried. I don't even know why; probably because whatever it was we once had didn't work. Then we stayed up till four in the morning with a bottle of cognac. Just before dawn, I came very close to calling the whole move off."

"And?"

"I decided that forgetting is a function of intervening experience; that Allen and I, both of us, will get over it; that

I had nothing more to say to him other than I thought he was a good person and I hoped he had a good life.'' Just for a moment, she drew back, deep in thought. "Tom, I don't want to talk about Allen anymore. This is the rest of my life.''

The hours passed, and we talked. About parents and lovers, teachers and friends, all the forces that had shaped our lives. Through it all, I sensed a growing closeness and the feeling that maybe I'd been right about the two of us nine months earlier when we'd met. After all that time, there was still a touch of magic between us.

Laura's head dipped to my shoulder.

"Did you bring a toothbrush?'' she asked, somewhere in the neighborhood of 3:00 A.M.

"I thought about it, but I was afraid you'd think I was being presumptuous.''

"You can use mine, if you like.'' Taking my hand, she stood up and led me to the bedroom, coming to a halt by the bed. "You know what I like about you?'' she said.

"I give up; what?''

"The way you undress. Most men take their shoes and pants off first, which makes them look like Walter Matthau or Steve Martin. Whenever we make love, you start with your shirt.'' Reaching down, she turned back the blanket and top sheet. "Incidentally, in case you feel something crumbly, last night I was eating cookies in bed.''

Slowly, in some ways as though it were the first time, we began to make love—excited, a little nervous, both of us mindful that something had changed. Somehow, though we'd been lovers for months, I'd lost sight of who Laura was. Maybe my fascination for The Fantasy Jogger had left me blind. Maybe the constraint of knowing that Laura always had to get up and go home to her husband had taken a toll. Or maybe this was a new woman, free at last from a marriage that had wasted her spirit and assaulted her soul.

"Hey, Tom. It's nice to be spending the whole night with someone I'm excited about. It's been a long time."

Sunday morning, we slept until noon, before going out for brunch and visiting a museum afterward. Laura had already made plans for dinner, so, late in the day, I took her home, then went back to my apartment. That night I picked up *The Mariah Project* from my typist, and, for the first time, read the manuscript through from beginning to end. At first I was nervous about whether the plot would hold together; but, as I read on, it was clear that the book worked. All it needed was a little polishing and a few minor revisions before being placed in the capable hands of Augustus Hasson.

Monday, I went to the Fordham Law Library to put the final touches on my magnum opus. For the first time since our midnight rendezvous, I saw Kathy Hart, who pretended not to see me. Around noon, I had coffee with Sylvia Pennock in the school cafeteria.

"It was a one-time experiment," Sylvia advised in a friendly sort of way without my having to ask. "But I enjoyed it. Someday, when you're a famous author, I plan on telling people at cocktail parties that I knew you when you were writing *The Mariah Project*."

"Fair enough. And if you make it to the United States Supreme Court, I'll do the same." Our eyes met, and it occurred to me that Sylvia and I had developed an odd but nice friendship. "Let me ask you something. Are you and Kathy happy together?"

Looking a trifle self-conscious, Sylvia tugged at the cuff of her shirt. "We have our problems, like other couples. If we didn't, we wouldn't have invited you to our apartment."

"But are you happy?"

"We're working on it. You have to understand, I've decided it's important for me to make up my own mind in life and not let other people do it for me."

We talked for an hour, then went back to the library. A day later, *The Mariah Project* was complete—390 pages, a year of my life. Too anxious to wait for my typist, I typed the revisions myself. Next stop, Augustus Hasson—but not yet. Something inside—I wasn't sure what—was holding me back. Again, I read the manuscript through from start to finish. Everything was there. But there was one more necessary step.

That night, Big Walter and I went out for dinner, choosing as we often did to dine at Imbalzhno's. "I've got a trivia question for you," he announced as we took our seats. "How are the stars arranged on an American flag?"

"Five rows with six stars each, alternating with four rows of five."

For a moment, there was silence.

"I'm flabbergasted," he admitted. "How in the world did you know that?"

"I'm a patriotic American. Besides, I ran into Patricia at the supermarket this morning, and she told me you asked her the same question last night."

For the next few minutes, we reminisced about old sports figures and rock-and-roll hits. Then the conversation turned serious.

"There's something I'd like you to do for me," I said.

"Speak and it's yours."

More apprehensive than I thought I'd be, I made my request: "Big Walter, *The Mariah Project* is finished. I like it. In fact, I like it a lot, but I'm scared stiff. All of a sudden, I'm worried no one will see what I want them to see in it; or the plot doesn't work; that David Barrett is a nebbish; that Carolyn Hewitt is all in my mind. I want you to read it, and then I want you to be honest. This might be the hardest thing I'll ever ask of our friendship, but, if the book stinks, I want to hear it from you first, not from Augustus Hasson.''

For longer than I care to remember, Big Walter was silent. ''All right,'' he said at last, a touch of worry clouding his face. ''I'll do it.''

Neither of us had much to say for the rest of dinner. When the meal ended, we went back to my apartment and I gave him the manuscript.

''Remember! I want the truth.''

Maybe it was an unfair burden to lay on his shoulders. But, if there was bad news ahead, Big Walter was the person I trusted to tell it. ''Hammond,'' I told myself around midnight as I lay in bed, ''you've put a lot of eggs in your literary basket. Let's hope they don't break.''

Five hours later, well before dawn, the telephone rang. Bleary-eyed, disoriented, I picked up the receiver.

''I just finished *The Mariah Project*,'' Big Walter announced. ''It's fantastic. I mean, I'm not bullshitting you. It's one of the most exciting books I've ever read.''

In everyone's life, there are certain high points forever remembered. For me, Big Walter's call was one of those moments. Strange as it might sound, I hadn't realized the anxiety and tension that had built up inside as I'd worked on *The Mariah Project*. Now the first review was in, and it was good. That morning, twenty minutes before the neighborhood Xerox shop opened, I was standing outside with the manuscript. By noon, a finished copy had been delivered to the East Side town house of Augustus Hasson.

''He's very busy,'' Marcia Steinberg advised, explaining why I couldn't hand my masterpiece to The Great One in person. ''But I'm certain he'll read it and get back to you as soon as possible.''

That afternoon, I had lunch with Laura. Then I rolled $20

worth of pennies I'd collected in an old cookie jar over the past few years and went to the bank. A dozen people were in line ahead of me. At least fifteen minutes passed before I got to a teller.

"I'd like to turn these in for a twenty-dollar bill."

"You got an account here?" the teller queried.

"Yes, sir."

Eyeing the rolls (forty of them, fifty pennies each), the young man whose job it was to assist customers made a face. "I can't take them."

"Why not?"

"You have to write your name, address, telephone number, and account number on each one. That way, if you're a penny short, we can deduct it from your account."

The woman next on line began making noises for me to hurry up. Incredulously, I stared at the teller. "Are you telling me I have to write all that on forty separate rolls of pennies?"

"That's what I said."

"You can't be serious."

"I'm sorry, this is a bank. If someone shortchanges us, we have to even up the account."

"And what if there's a penny extra? Does that mean you'll credit my account?"

"I wouldn't know. That's another department."

The line was growing. Only one other teller was on duty.

"Look," I suggested. "Why don't we do this: I'll write my name, address, telephone number, and account number on one roll. If you'd like, I'll also inscribe my Social Security number and place of birth. Then, at the end of the day, if you have nothing better to do, you can write it on the other thirty-nine."

For about ten seconds, we exchanged looks.

"All right. But, next time, follow the rules or else we won't be able to take your pennies."

That was my confrontation for the week. The following morning, Augustus Hasson's secretary called to confirm that my manuscript would be read within ten days "or as soon after as possible." Catching up on neglected housework, I cleaned two closets and repotted a dozen plants. Then I went shopping for underwear and shirts. Over the preceding few months, I'd let slip a number of ministerial matters. Columbia University Press had written to solicit an essay for an upcoming anthology on William Jennings Bryan. A student forum had scheduled a series of panel discussions on American political history, and wanted to know if I'd participate. One by one, I considered the requests, agreeing to some, declining others. The last thing I wanted was a full set of academic obligations. With *The Mariah Project* complete, I'd begun to undergo a personal decompression of sorts. After living with my characters day and night for nine months, their departure had left me washed out, maybe even a little depressed.

For several days, I mulled over potential commitments, wondering what I should do and what to write next. The whole world seemed unusually grim. Why? What reason? And then it hit: David Barrett, Carolyn Hewitt, all of my creations were now dead. For others who might someday read the book, they would come alive; but all that was left for me was the memory of a long-lost friend and lover. *Carolyn Hewitt was gone. I'd never see her again.*

"Maybe it's for the best," Big Walter told me that night. "Now you can concentrate on real people."

Maybe. But part of me sensed I'd never be that enchanted again. And sometimes, even now, when I look back on those days with Carolyn Hewitt, I take solace in words penned a century ago by Charles Dickens in the preface to *David Copperfield*, where Dickens wrote:

> I do not find it easy to get sufficiently far away from this book in the first sensations of having finished it to refer to it with composure. My interest in it is so recent and strong that I am in danger of wearying the reader with personal confidences and private emotions. It would concern the reader little, perhaps, to know how sorrowfully the pen is laid down at the close of a two-years' imaginative task; or how an author feels as if he were dismissing some portion of himself into the shadowy world, when the creatures of his brain are going from him forever. Yet I have nothing else to tell, unless indeed I were to confess that no one can ever believe this narrative in the reading more than I have believed it in the writing. Therefore, I close with a hopeful glance toward the time when I shall again put forth my two green leaves once a month, and with a faithful remembrance of the genial sun and showers that have fallen on these leaves of *David Copperfield* and made me happy.

13

WITH *The Mariah Project* complete, Patricia decreed that a celebration was in order. Ergo, she spent two days preparing a gourmet dinner for Laura, Big Walter, and me. Early in the evening, we talked about the art of screenwriting and whether or not women should pay for themselves on dates. Then came a variety of hors d'oeuvres followed by leek salad and striped bass with green sauce. The pièce de résistance was an incredible homemade concoction referred to as "King Arthur's chocolate cake."

Big Walter ate three pieces.

"If you eat any more," Patricia warned, "we'll have to change your name from Big Walter to Fat Walter."

Whereupon Big Walter ate the last piece.

"There were three reasons you shouldn't have done that," his devoted wife counseled. "One, you'll keep me up all night complaining your stomach is stretched. Two, you of all people don't need two thousand more calories. And three, I wanted to eat it myself tomorrow for breakfast.''

After coffee, we contemplated the nation's political state and weighed the accuracy of media news coverage. Patricia volunteered that she thought Dan Rather was kind of cute but Roger Mudd seemed more reliable. Big Walter lamented the change in campus political values: ''When we were in school, we were concerned with social justice and Vietnam. Now the main issue on college campuses seems to be the availability of student parking.''

''It's a different era,'' Laura answered. ''Today's students aren't in danger of being drafted.''

Sometime around 11:00, we opened a bottle of brandy. ''I'll never forget my one acting experience,'' Patricia reminisced. ''I was in third grade, and my class put on a play for Christmas. My only line was 'Warm milk, ugh!' ''

''When I was in third grade,'' Big Walter remembered, ''the prettiest girl in class sat three rows behind me. I had this incredible crush on her, to the point where I remember fantasizing that we were grown-ups engaged to be married.''

''God, I was brilliant!'' Patricia continued. '' 'Warm milk, ugh!' Sarah Bernhardt must have turned over in her grave with envy when she heard that.''

Much later, Laura and I tottered back to my apartment and readied for bed. By prearrangement, she had dropped off a nightgown and sundry other items before dinner. Much like an established couple, we brushed our teeth, changed into nightclothes, and crawled between the sheets.

''They're a nice couple,'' Laura said. ''The whole room seems to light up when Big Walter and Patricia are together.''

For a while, we traded notes on the evening just past, then moved to the present.

''Since this is our first overnight at your apartment,'' Laura queried, ''I have to ask—are you one of those people who goes to bed at night, takes off his pajamas to make love, and puts them back on again when he's finished? Because, if you are, you should be advised that it's like rewrapping a Christmas present after it's been opened.''

Appropriately forewarned, I reached below the hem of her nightgown and ran my hand to her waist. Pressing her body against mine, she touched my lips with a kiss.

"You know something?" I said. "Sometimes I lose sight of how beautiful you are. Whatever you wear, whatever the look, it's as though you don't even have to work at it.''

"You're marvelously naïve," she answered. "Believe me, it takes work.''

"Does it?"

"Nonstop. I exercise; I diet; I won't tell you what it costs to have my hair cut. If I dress down, it's because I've seen what happens to women who bask in favors because of their looks. She who lives by the sword dies by it. There's no way a woman of forty can compete with women of twenty-five on a looks basis, particularly in the media business, so I'm building for what lies ahead. Besides,'' she added, running a finger across my chest, "people notice when I want them to notice.''

The cold days of February moved on inexorably. Much to my annoyance, I came down with the flu and spent three days in bed. Patricia suggested that Big Walter be hung in effigy when the building boiler broke for the third time in a month. A Hollywood starlet named Erica Quackenbos (whose literary agent was none other than Augustus Hasson) authored a book titled *Strawberries at Midnight*. "Miss Quackenbos," reported *The New York Times Book Review*, "recounts in vivid detail her romantic trysts with such notables as Burt Reynolds and Warren Beatty. In essence, she is being rewarded by the literary public for throwing up and then writing about it." *Strawberries at Midnight* promptly zoomed to number one on the best-seller list, and was auctioned off in paperback for $1.4 million.

Toward the end of February, I succumbed to the entreaties of Columbia University Press and agreed to write an essay on "William Jennings Bryan and the Campaign of 1896." Within days, "free silver," the "Cross of Gold" oration, and Mark Hanna were second nature to me. "God, you're versatile," Sylvia Pennock observed one afternoon in the Fordham Law Library. "What's next?"

"I wish I knew," I conceded. "A lot depends on what happens with *The Mariah Project.*"

"Have you heard from your agent?"

"Not yet."

Four more days went by, making it a total of three weeks since I'd handed the manuscript to The Great One's office assistant. Several times, I thought of calling, but——

"Wait a while," Laura counseled. "With someone of Augustus's stature, you have to allow at least a month."

The days passed. Patricia was promoted to chief buyer for the leather-goods wholesale office where she worked. The long-awaited *RFK's Women* by Edwin Smyth appeared in print. Big Walter suggested that, if things with the novel didn't work out, I could always go into business free-lancing suicide notes. On February 28, the last day of winter's coldest month, I returned home from a day in the library and played back the messages on my telephone-answering machine: "Mr Hasson has read your book," a voice said. "Be here to discuss it tomorrow morning at ten o'clock."

That night, all over again, I got nervous. Whatever it was The Great One wanted to discuss, I wished his secretary had disclosed it. "Mr. Hasson loved your novel; Mr. Hasson feels that substantial rewriting will be necessary on the second part; Mr. Hasson thinks the book stinks!'' Couldn't she have given a hint of what to expect!

The next morning, promptly at 10:00, I arrived at Augustus Hasson's East Side town house. A thin layer of snow from the night before lay on the city's streets. Marcia Steinberg opened the front door and, exuding the charm of a woman roller-derby skater, led me to the waiting room, where a secretary sat typing. Everything seemed the same as it had eight months earlier, except that the number of dust jackets on the wall had increased incrementally.

''Please be seated,'' Ms. Steinberg instructed.

Several minutes passed. Catching sight of my reflection in the glass-covered frame that celebrated *Kennedy's Women,* I waved, more in homage to JFK than as a means of saying hello to myself. Another assistant, young with the warmth of a blonde Barbie Doll, emerged from the inner office and looked toward me. ''I'd like you to ask me out,'' her half-smile said, ''but only so I can say no.''

''Mr. Hasson will see you now. His office is through the door straight ahead.''

Like the waiting room, the inner office was substantially unchanged. The huge glass-topped desk was still uncluttered. The white-lacquered shelves housed the same array of books. Beyond the window, an inch of snow covered the patio area, giving rise to the question of where The Great One would eat lunch; but otherwise his routine seemed unthreatened by the passage of time. As before, the world's greatest literary agent was seated at his desk. His face was tan, indicating a journey south and, as always, it was well fed. Without standing, he gestured for me to sit opposite the desk. The telephone buzzed, and he ignored it.

''I've read your book,'' Augustus Hasson began, punctuating his introductory remark with a pause that seemed unduly dramatic. . . . ''There's a talent to writing, and you have it.

The Mariah Project is wonderfully commercial and not without literary merit.''

A sigh of relief escaped my lips. Looking quite satisfied with the manner in which he had played the drama, The Great One leaned back and rubbed his hands together.

"Your woman character is particularly well developed. In some ways, she raises the manuscript above the level of a genre potboiler. You owe her a considerable debt."

I waited, confident that the commentary would continue without prompting on my part.

"Marketing a first novel is tricky business. Anne Tolstoi Wallach received $850,000 for *Woman's Work,* but that was unique. Last year, I sold a first novel to Random House for six figures. However, as you know, I deal primarily with established writers, so I won't hazard an estimate on your book. I'll simply say that, with your manuscript and my skill as an agent, we should do quite nicely together." Reaching out, he stabbed at the intercom. "Miss Altner, please bring me the usual copies of the agency contract."

Moments later, the Barbie Doll appeared, bearing two mimeographed sheets.

"This contract," Hasson began, gesturing toward the sheets, "will constitute the full agreement between us. I'd like you to sign both copies and leave them with Ms. Altner on your way out."

"Could I read it first?"

"If you wish."

Taking the top sheet, I glanced at the heading—"THE MARIAH PROJECT." Below that, the contract read:

Author hereby empowers The Augustus Hasson Literary Agency to act as his exclusive Agent in connection with all matters relating to the above-titled work. Author hereby irrevocably assigns and transfers to the Augustus

Hasson Literary Agency ten percent (10%) of all monies paid to Author on account of said work (except that, with respect to foreign publication rights, Agent's commission shall be twenty percent). Author agrees to include this contract in any agreement for compensation to him relating to the above-titled work. All monies due hereunder to Agent or Author shall be paid to and in the name of The Augustus Hasson Literary Agency, 303 East 54th Street, New York, N.Y., 10022.

"I trust, Mr. Hammond, that the contract is to your liking."

"Yes, sir."

"Very well, then. If you'll sign both copies, we can get on with the business of selling your book."

Leaning forward, I rested both sheets on the desk. The ebullient Ms. Altner handed me a Dunhill fountain pen and I signed twice, inscribing my name with a curl in the "T" for posterity's sake.

"On second thought," Hasson said, turning to his assistant, "why don't you take the contracts to the file room now? That way, we'll save Mr. Hammond the trouble of carrying them out." Then, looking quite content, he directed his attention back toward me. "Tom—I hope you don't mind my calling you Tom—how much money did you make last year as a professor at Columbia?"

"Not much," I admitted. "Somewhere in the neighborhood of twenty——"

Waving his hand, The Great One cut me off. "No matter. I know how things are in academia. Let's turn *The Mariah Project* into a million dollars."

14

LOOKING BACK ON my first year as a writer, I'm struck by how little time I actually spent with Augustus Hasson. Our initial meeting, when he reviewed my proposal for *The Mariah Project*, lasted less than ten minutes. Our second encounter was even briefer. Still, by skill, reputation, and force of personality, he dominated like an Oriental potentate. Now it was time for the potentate to find a publisher for my novel, and the manner in which he went about it was highly instructive.

If all goes well, authors receive money from three sources. First and foremost is the hardcover advance. Each hardcover publisher gives its authors "x" dollars set against royalties on the sale of a book. Generally, royalties are paid on a sliding scale—10 percent of list price for the first 5,000 copies sold, 12½ percent on the next 5,000, and 15 percent thereafter. Thus, if an author gets a hardcover advance of

140

$5,000 on a $10 book, and the book sells 2,500 copies, royalties are 2,500 times $1, for a grand total of $2,500. Since the advance was twice that amount, the book hasn't "earned out." The author keeps the extra money and gets nothing more. On the other hand, if the book sells 50,000 copies in hardcover, royalties on a sliding percentage would equal $71,250. Since the author was paid $5,000 initially, he (or she) gets an additional $66,250.

The next potential source of revenue is the paperback market. About 20 percent of all books that come out in hardcover find their way into paper. Here again, an advance against royalties is negotiated, although the royalty percentages are somewhat less. Then, if the author is truly fortunate, miscellaneous income is added from film producers, the sale of book excerpts to magazines, etc. On those rare occasions when everything goes right, writing can be extremely lucrative.

Once a book is written, there are several ways an agent can sell it. Established authors frequently find it preferable (and profitable) to stay with the publisher who made them famous. Thus, when Graham Greene writes a book, his agent sits down and talks turkey with Simon & Schuster. Ditto for James Michener with Random House, John LeCarré at Alfred Knopf, and so on. But for first novelists (and most other writers), that luxury doesn't exist. Thus, agents often resort to what is known as an "auction."

The biggest advantage auctions offer is that they're quick. An agent sends copies of his author's manuscript to a number of publishers with a covering letter that specifies an auction date. Interested publishers then bid on the appropriate day, and, one by one, the low bidders are given an opportunity to raise the ante. Ultimately, the highest dollar offer prevails. It's efficient, and manuscripts submitted by premier agents frequently engender substantial interest. Thus, it was with considerable pleasure, several days after my visit with Au-

gustus Hasson, that I opened my mail and found the following note.

Dear Tom,

The Mariah Project has been sent to the following
publishers: Atheneum, Crown, Doubleday, Dutton, Har-
court, Harper & Row, Little Brown, McGraw-Hill, Mor-
row, Putnam, Random House, Scribner's, Simon &
Schuster, Viking, and Wallace Press.

The auction will be held three weeks from today, on
March 24.

Sincerely,
Augustus Hasson

On receiving the letter, I telephoned Marcia Steinberg to
see if The Great One wanted me in his office on the auction
date.

"Goodness, no!" came the response. "As things develop,
we'll keep you posted."

"What might develop?"

"Just the usual—some early turndowns; one or two pre-
liminary bids."

Satisfied that the matter was in good hands, I returned to
Fordham to finish work on "William Jennings Bryan and the
Campaign of 1896." Overall, I enjoyed the task, but my
enthusiasm for academia had dwindled.

"What do you think you'll do next?" Sylvia Pennock asked
one afternoon, repeating what had become her favorite query.

"Another novel, but I'll need some new characters and a
vacation first."

"How big an advance will you get for *The Mariah Project*?"

"That's hard to say," I told her. "For hardcover, forty,
maybe fifty thousand dollars."

That night, I raised the figure to fifty flat. The following morning, in the mail, I received a memo "From the Desk of Augustus Hasson." Affixed with a paper clip were letters from Simon & Schuster and Scribner's:

Dear Augustus,

Thanks so much for letting me see *The Mariah Project*. Thomas Hammond is good; there's no doubt of that. But our thriller list is already complete and it's awfully tough these days to break in a new author.

Dear Augustus,

Hats off! You've come up with another blockbuster. Unfortunately, we simply can't see our way through to paying the type of advance we know you'd expect. But best of luck to you and Hammond.

"Don't worry," read the handwritten scrawl across the memo sheet, "there are thirteen left—A. H."

March progressed as always, cold but with the tantalizing promise of spring ahead. Big Walter finished another screenplay—this one about a mutiny by Russian sailors on board a Soviet submarine. Laura decided that her midnight to 8:00 A.M. schedule at NBC was unacceptable now that she and Allen had split. "The truth is, graveyard hours were an escape," she confided one night. "When Allen slept, I was at work. When Allen was free, I was asleep." Later in the week, she applied for and received a transfer to the daytime shift. Coincidental with the change, two more rejections came in on *The Mariah Project*:

Dear Augustus,

Thomas Hammond has a flair for writing but, for me, *The Mariah Project* doesn't quite work. I know you'll prove me wrong again—you old codger—but this time we'll pass.

Dear Augustus,

Thanks a lot for sending me Thomas Hammond's *The Mariah Project*. I liked it, as did several others here, but somehow it falls a bit short. He's such a fine storyteller, though, I hope you'll keep me in mind for anything else he might write.

That night, I went out for dinner with Big Walter and Patricia.

"Keep your chin up," Big Walter counseled. "After all, you knew from the start that not everyone would bid."

"I guess so," I admitted. "But still, I feel a little like someone who's been rejected after a blind date—How did you like her? Oh, she was very nice. Are you planning to ask her out again? No!"

After dinner, we went back to my place for coffee and cake.

"Remember," Patricia cautioned, "only one piece."

Looking less than thrilled by the caveat, Big Walter seated himself at the kitchen table. "I told you," he said, glaring at his wife, "everyone has to find a weight they're comfortable with. Whenever I fall below two-sixty, I feel sickly and lose my balance."

Rolling her eyes, Patricia looked toward me for help. "Tom, be honest. You're Big Walter's best friend. Don't you think he should go on a diet?"

"Tom's opinion has nothing to do with it," Big Walter

grumbled. "This is between the two of us. I'm fully aware of the difference between being a gourmet and being a glutton; nowhere was it written on Mount Sinai that you can't eat ice cream for breakfast; and, in the immortal words of Jean-Paul Sartre, diet soda tastes like piss. I believe that covers all the bases, except I see nothing wrong with eating raw chocolate-chip-cookie batter for dinner like I did last night. The key is knowing when to stop, so you don't get sick." His piece spoken, Big Walter looked at me with a benign, almost saintly visage. "By the way, if you have any fruit in the refrigerator, I'll take that instead of cake."

Another week passed. With my essay on William Jennings Bryan complete, I agreed to revise a textbook for Columbia University Press. Laura decided that daytime hours were to her liking. Rejection number five (this one from Doubleday) came in on *The Mariah Project*. "Don't worry," I told myself. "You've got the best agent in the business." Still, the reality of five turndowns without a nibble was troubling, and, with the pressure mounting, I began to think in terms of a vacation as a diversion to more pleasant times ahead. In years past, I'd traveled through most of the United States. Now something more exotic seemed right.

"India," I announced one night as Laura and I were readying for bed. "Four weeks, maybe five, sometime this summer. I'd love it if we could go together."

Just for a moment, I thought she'd accept. The Taj Mahal was glimmering in her eyes.

"I don't know," she said. "Right now, the timing is bad. Too many things are happening at work, and I have some very basic decisions to make with my life." Then, sensing my disappointment, she gave me a hug. "Tom, you're very important to me; you know that. But I can't put you in Allen's place and, whatever it is you and I have together, it has to go slowly. I can't handle an overload of intimacy yet."

*   *   *

As the month wore on, Big Walter's diet showed no noticeable effect. *Time* magazine reported that *RFK's Women* and *Strawberries at Midnight* were running one-two on the best-seller list. Patricia got another raise at work. Sylvia Pennock and Kathy Hart decided to split up.

"Them's the breaks," Sylvia said as she told me of the dissolution over our ritual cup of coffee in the Fordham cafeteria. "If you know any women, give them my number."

The first day of spring came and went. Another rejection arrived on *The Mariah Project*:

Dear Augustus,

Thanks for letting me have a look at Thomas Hammond's first novel. It's quite exciting, but I really didn't find the idea of energy-saving crystals plausible.

One day later, Marcia Steinberg called to report turndowns from Viking and Putnam. One wanted more specifics on Middle East political issues, the other less.

Eight down; seven left.

Bright and early on Auction Day (March 24), I woke up, shaved, showered, and scrambled some eggs. A few minutes before ten, the telephone sounded. "Good luck," Big Walter exhorted. "Knock 'em dead."

10:00 . . . 11:00 . . . Anxiously, I scanned the list I'd prepared on a sheet of yellow paper the previous night:

Atheneum	
Crown	
Doubleday	no
Dutton	
Harcourt	no

Harper & Row	
Little Brown	no
McGraw-Hill	
Morrow	no
Putnam	no
Random House	
Scribner's	no
Simon & Schuster	no
Viking	no
Wallace Press	

Just before noon, I picked up the phone and, for the first time ever, dialed Augustus Hasson's number.

"This is Tom Hammond," I told the secretary who answered. "Is Mr. Hasson in?"

"Could I ask what this is in reference to?"

"He's auctioning my book."

Following the expected "just a minute," I was put on hold. Then——

"Hi, Tom. This is Marcia Steinberg. Nothing yet."

"Nothing?"

"Only the turndowns. But don't worry. There's three left."

"I thought there were seven."

"Just a minute; let me check. . . . No, three is right. Crown, Harper & Row, Atheneum, and McGraw-Hill all said no this morning."

1:00 . . . 1:30 . . . Just before 2:00, Big Walter telephoned.

"Nothing's happened," I said. "I'll call you back, I promise. But I have to stay off the phone, just in case."

"Listen, have you had lunch yet?"

"How can I eat lunch? I'm ready to throw up."

"Take it easy," he said, acknowledging the desperation in my voice. "Why don't I pick up a couple of sandwiches and keep you company? It wouldn't hurt."

Grateful for the thought, I said yes. Big Walter and several deli sandwiches arrived twenty minutes later.

"You look awful," he announced. "If you stood on a street corner in your present state, people who walked by would give you money."

2:00 . . . 2:30 . . . Again, the telephone—wrong number. . . . 3:30 . . . 3:45 . . .

Just after 4:00, the telephone rang: "Mr. Hasson calling," the secretary announced. "One moment, please!"

"It's him," I whispered, cupping my hand over the receiver. . . . "Hello! Yes, sir. . . . I understand. . . . What, but what happens if the last one doesn't bid? . . . All right; yes, sir; thank you."

Rubbing my face with the palm of my hand, I hung up. Big Walter waited.

"That was the world's greatest literary agent," I said. "Dutton and Random House just voted no. Wallace Press is the only one left."

"Did he say what happens if there's no bid?"

"Yeah. His exact words were, 'Tom, it's not the worst thing in the world to have an unpublished novel. Think of it as a course in creative writing."

"What about other publishers? Arbor House, Macmillan—there's plenty left."

"He didn't mention it."

The next hour was a long one: maybe the longest of my life.

David Barrett . . . Carolyn Hewitt . . . All in my mind; that's all they'd ever been; quite literally, figments of my imagination. The Fantasy Jogger was a writer. That's what she'd said the day we met. Maybe, if she were by my side, what was happening would be more tolerable. But that wasn't the way life worked. Even in myths, mere mortals never capture Venus. She sweeps in from the clouds and then ascends to heaven again.

"Big Walter, what am I going to do?"

"I don't know. You can teach, rewrite, start on another novel. All I can tell you is, I've been where you are. And, whatever happens, it's a good book."

Just after 5:00, the curtain came down on my first auction.

"Mr. Hasson calling," the secretary said.

"Hello, Tom. This is Augustus. How are you? . . . Fine, I'm glad to hear it. Not everyone takes these things as well as you do. There's a horrible misconception afloat in some circles that a top agent like myself can turn every book into a million dollars. As you know, neither I nor anyone else can do that."

Part of me wanted to say "fuck you" and hang up.

"We have an offer."

"What!"

"We have an offer, from Wallace Press. It's only sixty-five hundred, but, if the book catches on, the size of the advance is irrelevant. John Fowles got half that for *The Collector*. William Blatty sold *The Exorcist* for peanuts, and it made him rich. It's our only offer. I recommend that you accept it."

Success; bittersweet!

"Congratulations," Big Walter boomed when the call was over. "You've got a publisher, and I think that's fantastic."

15

THE AUCTION WAS a success. At least, that was one way of looking at it. I had a publisher, which is more than most authors can say, and by year's end I'd be in print. In some ways, I felt like a runner who falls, gets back up, checks himself, and finds no bones broken; bruises, maybe, but that was all.

"The contract with Wallace Press won't be ready for about a month," Augustus told me when the auction ended. "That's standard in publishing. The first thing an editor says once he's bought your book is that there's a backlog in the contract department."

The following afternoon, I received a telephone call from Brad Carlisle, the editor who had authorized purchase of my book. "I think it's great," Brad told me. "Give me a week to reread the manuscript, and then we can talk."

Buoyed by his enthusiasm (and remembering how close I'd

come to death), I celebrated by taking Big Walter and Patricia to dinner. Then I went to the New York City Public Library to do some research on Wallace Press.

Cyrus Wallace had been born in Boston to Brahmin wealth in 1874. After graduating from Harvard, he moved to New York and began work as an editorial assistant for John W. Lovell Publishers. Twenty years later, he founded the publishing house that bore his name. Shy and aloof, with a near-pathological desire for anonymity, Wallace was a man of solid business acumen and sound literary judgment. On the personal side, he wed for the first time at age fifty and fathered his only child two years later. His one visible self-indulgence was a gold chain affixed to his vest with a Phi Beta Kappa key and Hamilton pocket watch attached.

Outside of Max Perkins, who reigned at Scribner's from 1910 to 1946, Wallace was the most respected editor of his era, recognized by the authors he nourished as a giant. He believed that editors should be invisible, that their primary task was to inspire writers to new heights. Unlike many of his contemporaries, he considered it an article of faith that "a book belongs to the author." And he was altogether devoted to "good books."

"What's a good book?" he would often ask as an exercise in Socratic dialogue. "One that makes money? No! One that a reader hates to lay aside? No! A good book is one that has a long and lasting impact on life."

In 1954, at age eighty, Cyrus Wallace retired from publishing. Much to his embarrassment, five hundred admirers gathered for a testimonial dinner on his behalf and, at the close of ceremonies, the guest of honor was called upon to speak. His remarks were brief: "I knew it was time for me to retire when I noticed that those stuffy old men in *The New Yorker* cartoons looked much younger than I look. I only hope that, fifty years from now, history will record that Wallace Press published good books."

That was the legacy of Cyrus Wallace. After his death, Wallace Press (like the rest of publishing) grew more commercial, but the house maintained its reputation for editorial excellence. Pulitzer Prize nominations were not uncommon. Occasionally, a Wallace Press publication found its way onto the best-seller list.

"You're lucky," Laura told me when the auction was over. "It's a good place to start."

True to his word, Brad Carlisle telephoned a week after our first conversation to invite me for lunch. Just before noon on the appointed day, I arrived at Wallace Press and presented myself to the receptionist. The office, located in a modern high-rise on Third Avenue, bore little resemblance to what I'd imagined a publishing house would look like. Sleek white lines and a bright green carpet dominated the reception area. The sole concession to the memory of Cyrus Wallace was his name in raised gold letters opposite the entrance. Soon after my arrival, a pleasant-looking man of about thirty, tall and slender with light brown hair, came out to greet me.

"Hi! I'm Brad Carlisle. I loved your book." We shook hands, and, after a few pleasantries, he led me back past a row of cubicles to a small office overlooking the street. A large desk took up much of the floor. Behind that, shelves jammed with books obscured the wall. Brad seated himself behind the desk and, as he did, I reordered my image of what an editor was supposed to look like. Somehow, I'd expected an older man, an authority figure of sorts. Instead, here was someone my own age, maybe younger, perfectly nice, the sort of person I'd enjoy having a beer with.

"Let me tell you how I view our relationship," Brad said. "As an editor, I don't rewrite. That's your prerogative. As for changing the manuscript, I have a few suggestions, but they're only that. One or two points strike me as underdeveloped. Midway through Part Two, the plot gets a bit confusing. But it's your story and your opinion that counts. Fair enough?''

I nodded.

"I'm curious; how did you get Augustus Hasson to be your agent?''

"Through a friend."

"You're lucky. Augustus is a bit overbearing, but he's good. His submissions are consistently viable from a commercial point of view, and, God knows, he does well by his clients.''

"Let's hope so," I was tempted to answer. "I have to earn a living at this.''

"Editing is like a crossword puzzle." Brad continued, shifting gears somewhat. "I love it. So let me get to your book.'' Reaching toward a pile of papers, he extracted a manuscript recognizable as *The Mariah Project*. "First, I'll confirm what you probably know already. The story is exciting and well paced. At times, your descriptive passages are remarkably vivid. Last night, when I reread Chapter Eight, I could *see* the sky above Udaipur at night. And Carolyn Hewitt is fantastic. By the time I'd finished, I had something of a crush on her.''

Just for a moment, our eyes met.

"Anyway," Brad said, picking up where he'd left off, "you've got a first-rate book. After lunch, I'll give you my copy of the manuscript. There are several questions I've penciled in the margin and one or two passages you might want to rework. The only other suggestion I have regards the Law of Sea Treaty. Are you familiar with it?''

"A little bit.''

"All right. I think you should research it more fully and

include a page or two on what happens if it's ratified by the United States."

"Do you really think the treaty is relevant?"

"Maybe, maybe not. But it's worth the effort to find out. This is *your* book. And, come October, when it hits the streets, I want you to feel you've done everything possible to make it a success."

That night, I read through the comments Brad had made on *The Mariah Project.* Most of them were pretty good. "You're reading things into this scene that people won't see," he'd written at one juncture. In another chapter, he wanted more on David Barrett's emotional makeup. "And give Barrett a philosophy," the penciled notation concluded. "The wheel, the steam engine, electricity, oil—each of them changed the course of civilization. Barrett should be aware of the crystals' potential for doing the same. He wants to be a part of it."

For ten days, I reworked my plot; adding here, cutting there. Once or twice, I telephoned Brad to seek his advice. He was a good editor; his thoughts helped. Meanwhile, I began to think more seriously about a trip to India, and rejected Big Walter's offer to go into business together with a "dial-a-chocolate chip cookie recipe" telephone service.

"Why not?" Big Walter demanded.

"Because it's a stupid idea."

"No, it isn't. Look at 'Sports News' and 'Dial-a-Joke.' "

As we talked, sitting on the sofa in my apartment, I leafed through the morning mail. Augustus Hasson had finally gotten around to sending me the last batch of rejections on *The Mariah Project,* and I thought the letters might prove instructive:

Dear Augustus,

Thanks for sending me Thomas Hammond's recent manuscript. There's some good writing and I found it intriguing, but we've decided against putting in an offer.

One by one, I perused the letters. Then—"Hey, Big Walter. Look at this!"

Dear Augustus,

As you know, we've had great success with many of your books, including most recently *Strawberries at Midnight*. However, reading *The Mariah Project* was a bitter disappointment. Hammond's dialogue is contrived and clumsy. The book is lacking in many respects, most notably the absence of graphic sex. Given your eminence in the publishing industry, I fail to understand why you found it necessary to waste your time (and mine) with *The Mariah Project*.

Sincerely,
Richard Stoddart

"Screw him," Big Walter muttered—"Hey! Where are you going?"
"To my desk."
With Big Walter in close pursuit, I stomped to the bedroom and grabbed a piece of stationery from a box on the closet shelf. Then, grimly determined, I began to write:

Dear Mr. Stoddart,

Augustus Hasson was kind enough to forward your rejection letter of March 24. In response, I'm writing to tell you to go fuck yourself.

Obviously, not every book can measure up to your fine standards. After all, great literature like *Strawberries at Midnight* is hard to duplicate, and serious writers like Erica Quackenbos don't come along as often as we'd like. But those of us who toil in the literary vineyard keep on trying.

Under separate cover, I'll be sending you a copy of my next manuscript. Tentatively titled *Belt Buckle Broad,* it's about a large-breasted former cheerleader for the Dallas Cowboys who comes to New York and fucks a half-dozen building superintendents in an effort to find an apartment. One of the superintendents looks like Fidel Castro. I trust it will fit nicely with your autumn list.

Up your ass,
Thomas Hammond

Big Walter gazed over my shoulder as I wrote. "That's very funny," he said when I'd finished. "What are you planning to do with it?"

"Mail it."

"Not really!"

"Oh, no? Just watch."

Folding the letter, I reached for an envelope.

"Good luck," he murmured. "You're much braver—or far more foolish—than I ever thought."

On that note, I went back to my book. Previously, I'd considered the first draft a finished product, but Brad Carlisle's suggestions improved it markedly. By mid-April, the manuscript was virtually complete, and I decided to let it sit for a day or two before taking a final look. Meanwhile, as the weather turned fair, I resumed jogging on a regular basis, wondering if and when I'd catch sight of The Fantasy Jogger. As expected, she was nowhere in sight; and, after a few outings, I concluded that her absence was all for the best. Things with Laura were pretty good, and Carolyn Hewitt was far behind me. Better to get on with the rest of my life.

"You know something," Laura told me one night after a

candlelight dinner at her apartment. "Once upon a time, I was just using you to practice, but the two of us might have something together."

The thought was encouraging—so much so that I considered reissuing my invitation for a trip to India. But instinct told me the answer would still be negative.

"These are strange times," Laura said, continuing her thoughts. "Last year, leaving Allen was an end in itself. Now I'm beginning to realize it was only a beginning. Every day, another problem comes to the surface. Hiring a divorce lawyer, whether or not I should go back to my maiden name." A wistful look touched her face. "Once I'm divorced, Kinney wouldn't make sense. But professionally, and personally, for seven years I've been Laura Kinney."

Something in the air invited questions, but the time wasn't right.

"I thought about you the other night," Laura said. "I was in the shower washing my hair, and suddenly I had this marvelous image of you being followed around by a six-foot lined yellow pad. Somehow, all the men in my life have been yellow-pad fanatics. My father kept one on the edge of his desk when I was growing up. So did Allen, on the dresser. Actually, you and Allen are remarkably alike."

"How so?"

"Both of you are bright. You both have a low-key way of getting what you want. The difference is, you're more in touch with feelings—yours and mine—than Allen ever was. And you're more daring about life."

April progressed on a pleasant note. Four days after I turned in the revised manuscript, Brad Carlisle called to say it was "great." Soon after, a copy-edited version was messengered to my apartment. Reviewing the corrections, I noted several changes in spelling and punctuation, but nothing major. "All systems are go," Brad reported. "We'll send it to the printers and have galleys next month."

Meanwhile, Laura and I continued our random pattern of "dates." Generally, we saw each other several times a week, sometimes spending the night together, sometimes not. The abstentions were her choice, and recalled the dictum, "Whoever says no more often controls the relationship." Still, I resolved to be patient and wait.

"Allen called this afternoon," she announced one night. "He wanted to know if I'd meet him for dinner later in the week."

"What did you say?"

"I told him 'not yet.' "

Generally Laura avoided discussing her "ex." But now, for whatever reason, she wanted to talk.

"He calls at least twice a week. Sometimes at home, more often at work. The conversations are pretty forced."

"Have you told him about us?"

Letting her hair sweep past her shoulders, she shook her head. "Before I left, Allen asked if there was another man, and I told him no. Today he asked if I was dating anyone in particular, and I gave him the same answer. There are times when honesty is cruel and selfish."

"What will happen when he finds out?"

"He'll grieve; he'll cry. Then, hopefully, he'll get on with the rest of his life." Her voice trailed off. "Right now, he won't even date. I guess I'm afraid he'll always love me."

The next week was pretty quiet. Patricia decided she had a crush on Bjorn Borg. Big Walter invented a new game, which entailed lying on his back and rolling a marble into his belly button. Brad Carlisle called once or twice on minor matters having to do with the preparation of galleys and a printing schedule. On the last day of April, my contract arrived from Wallace Press, and I was summoned to meet with Augustus Hasson.

"Go right in," his secretary said when I arrived at the office. "He's expecting you."

As usual, The Great One remained seated when I entered. Marcia Steinberg followed me in and stood by the desk. The ebullient Miss Altner—as I had come to think of Hasson's Barbie Doll assistant—was in a chair with her steno pad and several memoranda resting on her lap.

"It's too bad," Hasson said, pointing me toward a seat. "If two or three houses had bid on *The Mariah Project,* we might have gone up as high as fifty or sixty thousand dollars. Just last week, I sold a novel to Random House for five times that amount."

Absorbing the comment, I waited. The Great One handed one last sheet of paper to Miss Altner and dismissed her with a cursory "please copy that." Then he turned back in my direction, and the monologue continued.

"I guess most writers would be satisfied with your advance, and I'm sure you're pleased with it. But before you're paid, there's the matter of your contract with Wallace Press." Leaning forward, he reached for a manila folder and thrust it out. "Here; I'll need your signature on each of these copies."

"Could I read them first?"

"They're all the same. Go ahead if you'd like."

Opening the folder, I scanned page one of the contract:

AGREEMENT between THOMAS HAMMOND (hereinafter called "Author"), and WALLACE PRESS ("Publisher"). The Author and Publisher mutually agree as follows . . .

There followed a long list of provisions governing copyright protection, royalties, reprint rights, options, and the like. Wallace Press, in its infinite generosity, had agreed to give "Author" six free copies of "the book." Additional copies could be purchased at a discount of 40 percent off list price. Midway down page two, there was a clause that provided my royalty rate would be substantially reduced on copies sold to large chain stores at discounts of more than 50 percent.

"How come Dalton Books gets a larger discount than I do?"

"They're bigger than you are," Hasson answered.

So it went. . . . Remainder sales, first serial rights. Just above the signature line was a clause labeled "Author's Warranty":

> The Author warrants that he is the sole Author of the work; that the work is original and does not violate the right of privacy of any person; that it is not libelous; and that it does not infringe upon any statutory or common law copyright. In the event of any claim based upon an alleged violation of this warranty, Publisher shall have the right *at the expense of Author* to defend against same using counsel of its own choosing, and Author agrees to indemnify Publisher for any judgment or settlement made in connection with such claim or lawsuit.

"What does that mean?"

"It's boilerplate," Hasson answered. "You'll find it in all publishing contracts."

"Maybe so, but I'd still like to understand it."

With no explanation forthcoming, I read the provision a second time.

"Wait a minute! Does this mean that if some nut in Texas or Iowa sues for plagiarism or libel, I have to pay for the lawyers that Wallace Press hires?"

"That's what it says."

"But that could run into thousands of dollars."

Wearily, The Great One ran his fingers along the glass-topped desk.

"Tom, I've been in the business for thirty years. You have the same warranty clause as everyone else."

For about ten seconds, my future seemed to hang in the balance.

Marcia Steinberg waited. Augustus Hasson looked on like a not-very-loving father.

"All right. I'll sign, but I don't like it."

One by one, Ms. Steinberg took the contracts as I scrawled my John Hancock. "Don't worry," Hasson said when I'd finished. "I give you my assurance, there will be no cause for regret."

Sensing that our meeting was over, I stood up.

"By the way, Mr. Hammond. There's one further matter I wish to discuss. Please return to your seat."

Under a withering look, I did as ordered.

"I understand that you recently sent a letter of sorts to Richard Stoddart. Is that correct?"

Long pause. I'd forgotten about that.

"Yes, sir; it is."

"Did you by any chance keep a copy?"

"No, sir."

Just for a moment, Augustus Hasson's eyes seemed to twinkle. "That's too bad. We could have passed it around the publishing community and made you famous. Oh, well. Don't do it again."

That night, Laura and I went out to celebrate.

"I don't know what lies ahead," she told me when the evening ended. "But I'm willing to walk down the road a way with you. Just be patient. Give us a chance."

16

THE BOOK WAS written; the contract was signed; a year had passed since I'd been out of Manhattan. So I went to India. Someday, perhaps, when I'm older and wiser, I'll understand what I found.

Years ago, the Indian government decided to build an underground sewer from Bombay to the ocean. Huge sections of clay pipe were brought to the city. But before construction could begin, thousands of people moved into the pipe. They didn't have homes.

The holiest city in India is Benares. To die there is a sacred end. The streets of Benares are rutted mud, littered with bodies of the dead and old. The air is humid, heavy with flies. Beneath funeral pyres, wild dogs fight over pieces of flesh borne by the wind.

Open sewers crisscross the land. Sanitation as practiced in the modern world is virtually unknown. The stench of urine

162

pervades all. "Everything in India smells except the roses," it has been said. Yet, high in the mountains, one comes to Ajanta and Ellora—caves where Buddhist monks fashioned statues and frescoes rivaling Europe's finest cathedrals. In Agra, the Taj Mahal mocks an era when the rest of the world built with mud and stone. In India one sees what was, and wonders what happened to it all.

On the first day of June, I came home. Sweetheart that he is, Big Walter borrowed a car and met me at the airport.

"What looks like half a hamburger?" he wanted to know.

"I give up."

"The other half."

With friends like Big Walter, you take the good with the bad.

Back at my apartment, I waded through four weeks' worth of magazines, telephone messages, and mail. From *Time* magazine, I learned that America's newest best seller was *The Beautiful People Diet* by Susan Jasper—a woman so stupid she spelt her first same "Soozin." (Honest! That's the way it appeared on the dust jacket.) From my telephone-answering machine, I learned that Laura would be in San Francisco on business until week's end. From the mail, I ascertained that The Augustus Hasson Literary Agency operated with at least one previously unmentioned charge:

Dear Tom,

Enclosed is a check for $5,475. This represents your advance on *The Mariah Project minus the $375 cost of Xeroxing fifteen auction copies*. Needless to say, my commission has also been deducted.

Sincerely,
Augustus Hasson

There were bills, a few personal letters, solicitations from a dozen charities—and a package from Wallace Press:

Dear Tom,

Enclosed are the galleys on *The Mariah Project*. Please read them for typographical errors and other changes by June 10th.

Regards,
Brad Carlisle

Staring at the long strips of paper in front of me, I felt a chill run through my entire body. In galley form, the book was there. Translated into hardcover, it would be slightly more than 300 pages long.

The next two days were devoted to laundry, marketing, and paying bills. Then I brought the galleys to Fordham, where classes and exams had come to an end. The library was empty, the students gone.

"Proofreading for typos is boring," I told Big Walter when we went jogging that afternoon. "Particularly since I've already read the manuscript nine times."

"Pretend you're looking for the Ninas in Hirschfeld," he counseled. "Then it's fun. Besides, with all the people Wallace Press has reading galleys, there shouldn't be any typos."

"I know there shouldn't be. The question is whether or not there are."

Lumbering along, Big Walter digested the comment, then shifted subjects. "By the way, I've got a great idea for a magazine article: 'Why I Hate Computer Video Games.' Do you think it will sell?"

"I don't know. I suppose it depends on why you hate them."

"That's what I thought you'd say, inasmuch as you're a

cautious individual. Incidentally, guess what!'' (One can never guess what goes on in Big Walter's mind.) "It's not final, but it looks as though Patricia is going to Italy.''

"What!''

"To Italy. Most of her firm's leather goods are imported from Rome. Someone has to go on a buying trip next month, and her boss can't make it. Patricia is ninety percent sure the trip is hers.''

"That's fantastic! How long will she be gone?''

"Ten days. And, believe me, she's earned every minute of it. I'm just sorry I won't be along.''

That night, I finished proofreading *The Mariah Project* and telephoned Sylvia Pennock to say hello. Then I made a batch of chocolate-chip cookies and ate most of them before they'd cooled. Around 11:00, Laura called from San Francisco with a formal "welcome home,'' and reported she'd be gone a few days more. We talked for twenty minutes, after which she went to dinner, and, New York time being three hours later, I went to bed. The following morning, I brought the corrected galleys back to Wallace Press.

"Good things are happening,'' Brad announced in the reception area as we shook hands. We walked past cubicles, secretarial alcoves, and miscellaneous rooms until we reached his office. "It's the busy season,'' he said, alluding to a stack of manuscripts and papers piled high on his desk. "Lots of last-minute details before the summer lull sets in.'' Leaning forward, he reached for a letter beside the stack and slid it across the desk in my direction. "Take a look. This should give you an idea of what it's like to be an editor.''

Dear Mr. Carlisle,

Six weeks ago, I submitted my untitled novel to Wallace Press. Yesterday it was returned with a form letter bearing your signature. This letter claims my book is ''not suited to your needs.'' However, the two slips of paper I inserted at pages 347 and 582 respectively were not removed. YOU NEVER READ MY NOVEL!!! How can you reject a manuscript without reading it!!!

''What was the book about?''

''To be honest,'' Brad answered, ''I don't remember. Each year we get thousands of unsolicited manuscripts, and a surprisingly high percentage are terrible—religious tracts, paeans to the gold standard, irrefutable evidence that Adolf Hitler is alive in Taos, New Mexico. When an unsolicited manuscript comes in, it goes on what we call the slush pile, and anyone who feels like it takes a look. Usually one chapter is enough.''

I waited, and Brad went on.

''It bothered me at first. I figured some poor soul had spent thousands of hours putting his heart on paper and I had an obligation to read what he wrote. But after a while I realized that my professional responsibility is to professional authors. That brings me to *The Mariah Project*.'' Opening a folder, he glanced at a two-page computer printout. ''I'll get to numbers in a moment, but first let me tell you that the manuscript has been distributed in-house. Judy Folger, who's our director of subsidiary rights, thinks a book-club sale is possible. Our marketing department recommends a first printing of twenty thousand copies. No publisher can sell material the public doesn't want, but we think the public will want this one.''

So far, so good.

''Publication date is October first,'' Brad continued. ''That means finished books will be back from the printer and in stores by that date. Best sellers require a ripple effect and the stone in the pond usually comes from New York, so we'll pay special attention to our accounts in Manhattan. Needless to say, there are no guarantees, but *The Mariah Project* has the potential to become a best seller. All we need now is a photo of the author, which is one of the fringe benefits of writing. I'm told it's a marvelous ego trip to walk past a bookstore and see your photograph on a dust jacket in the window."

That afternoon, I reported to Big Walter, who agreed to serve as official photographer. Then I went shopping for a roll of film and had dinner with Sylvia Pennock, who bemoaned the difficulties inherent in reestablishing her social life AKH (after Kathy Hart). The next day, I altered my routine by jogging in the morning (no Fantasy Jogger) and eating an early lunch. Then, camera in hand, I went over to Big Walter's. Patricia was home with a mild sore throat. Big Walter was wandering around the apartment seminaked.

"Patricia, have you seen my green-and-white striped shirt—the one with the hole in the elbow?"

"Yes."

"Where is it?"

"In the broom closet, where I put it with the other rags next to the bucket and mop."

There followed a brief debate as to whether Big Walter was old enough to determine when his clothes should be discarded. Needless to say, Patricia won, after which Big Walter and I went picture-taking in the park.

"The film has thirty-six exposures," he noted. "Do you want me to take all thirty-six?"

"I guess so. If we get one good photograph out of the bunch, we'll be lucky."

An hour later, the task was complete, and we decided to visit the Central Park Zoo—and, in particular, the monkey house. Following that foray, we returned to the West Side, and I helped Big Walter repair a light fixture in the basement.

Then we had dinner with Patricia, who was feeling better, and I went home to watch television while they went to the movies. Around 9:00 the telephone rang.

"I'm back," announced Laura. "And it's been an interesting five weeks. Come over, and I'll tell you about it."

Before we did anything, we made love. I'd assumed we'd talk, have a drink, and, later on, go to bed—which shows how structured two people can become. Instead, I walked in the door, put my arms around her, and realized that (1) this was a woman I was exceptionally fond of, and (2) I'd missed her. Five weeks is a long time. I kissed her, and talking made no sense at all.

"Which way is the bedroom?"

"Mr. Hammond, you're exceedingly forward tonight."

"I know. It just occurred me to that I've missed you."

The bed was made with an antique patterned quilt on top. Laura's face was radiant. Images—that's what I remember most about making love that night. Short, sharp snapshot images. Laura lifting her arms. Her lips, her smile. And then, suddenly, in the middle of it all, just for a moment, she pulled back with her eyes, as though skirting the abyss of a long and treacherous fall.

The moment passed. Reaching an arm around my side, Laura drew closer.

"Don't worry," I wanted to say. "I won't hurt you."

But instead, I said nothing—and waited—only to be caught off guard, as she had done to me so many times.

"Tom, did you sleep with other women while I was gone."

"No . . . Why?"

"Because I slept with other men—two of them—when you were in India. And all month long, it seemed important for me to tell you about them."

Just for a moment, I'm not sure why, I thought of Allen.

"Are you still——" I started to ask, then faltered.

"Not anymore. One was a one-nighter. The other lasted a little longer, but it was obvious we had nothing in common. His main assets were good looks and the fact that I'd never gone out with anyone that rich before. On our first date, we went to Lutèce. On the second, he took me to La Grenouille. Then he invited me to Paris for a weekend."

"He sounds perfect."

"Don't be hostile. I didn't go. And I told you, it's over. Besides, if it makes you feel better, he was just as inadequate as the rest of us. Whenever he got nervous, he'd tug at his hair the way an insecure person might twist a gold chain. Halfway through our third date, he had an anxiety attack and confessed that he thought I was more interesting than he was."

"What did you tell him?"

"I thought about it, and then I told him he was right. That sort of put a damper on the relationship. Anyway, I thought you should know. One of the reasons I left Allen was to go out with other men. And, in some ways, I felt abandoned when you went off to India. Whatever the reason, at least now I can feel we're honest with each other. And besides, the experience taught me a valuable lesson."

"What's that?"

"Being single is like having a second job, and the hours suck. But, to get back on point, maybe what I've been doing these past few months is healing scars and tying up loose ends. And maybe now I'm ready to reach out a little more in your direction than I have before."

And then Laura reached out in a way she'd never done before: "Tom, there's something I'd like. . . . Can I read *The Mariah Project*?"

17

WRITING A NOVEL is a more personal endeavor than most people realize. Sometimes the author models characters on himself. Other times, his subjects are fashioned from whole cloth. Either way, the book has a message to tell. That's not to say that *The Mariah Project* was loaded with insight. To the contrary, it was first and foremost an escapist thriller. But the manuscript did provide occasional commentary on world politics. And certainly, when it came to personal revelations, Carolyn Hewitt was close to my heart. Sharing the book with Laura before publication was an act of trust, but I was glad she'd asked. Two days later, I delivered the manuscript, neatly packaged in a ribbon-wrapped box. "I'll read it with care," she promised.

Meanwhile, Patricia's boss okayed her trip to Italy and set the date for early July. Big Walter finished another screenplay and began work on "Why I Hate Computer Video

Games.'' The literary world was stunned to learn that a post-humously published novel by best-selling author Byron Gouck had actually been written by Gouck's secretary after the putative author had died. Then, just when the furor seemed ready to subside, it was revealed that the same secretary had ghosted Gouck's previous five best sellers. A new diet book hit the top of the charts. *The White Diet,* as it was known, consisted exclusively of white-meat chicken, white rice, mashed potatoes, vanilla ice cream, white bread, cream cheese, certain kinds of noodles, and other things white.

While all this was going on, I spent my days in the library revising a textbook for Columbia University Press. In between, I managed to pick out a photo for *The Mariah Project* dust jacket and go jogging on a regular basis. Laura reported in glowing terms on *The Mariah Project,* and wondered aloud how I'd managed to piece together my plot.

''Index cards,'' I told her.

Duly impressed with The Hammond Method, she turned her attention to another item: ''Your heroine is an incredible woman. At times, she made me a bit jealous. Just don't forget. I'm real, she isn't.''

Part of me wanted to confess then and there; to warn Laura that she was competing with the image of a perfect woman. But, like the memory of a long-lost love, The Fantasy Jogger was best forgotten. Big Walter put the matter in perspective for me later that night: ''If you tell Laura now,'' he cautioned, ''putting the toothpaste back in the tube will be a very difficult matter.''

June moved on with a series of muggy, airless days that made Manhattan less than enjoyable. Brad Carlisle forwarded the jacket flap copy he'd written for *The Mariah Project.* Then, just before the July 4th weekend, he called to report that the dust jacket illustration was ready, and I journeyed to the offices of Wallace Press to take a look.

"How do you like it?"

Stepping back, I studied the layout. Three figures were set against a background of white. Two of them—obviously meant to be David Barrett and Carolyn Hewitt—were in the foreground, with Kaleel Rashad lurking behind. The title appeared in large block letters on top. Inscribed in smaller print at the bottom was the legend "by Thomas Hammond."

"I don't know. To be honest, it looks a little junky, like a paperback original. And Carolyn Hewitt's hair shouldn't be that dark. The book says it's light brown, not brunette."

Weighing my observations, Brad seemed partly sympathetic and a little annoyed. "Tom," he said, "have you ever heard of Patricia Granger?"

Shaking my head, I indicated I hadn't.

"Well let me tell you about her. Patricia Granger writes paperback originals. Over the past four years, she's written ten straight million-selling historical romances. Her husband, by the way, has written over one hundred novels. That might not be your idea of great literature, but she's a very talented woman at what she does, and one of the reasons her books sell is their covers. There's a much larger market out there for genre thrillers than erudite literature. If you want your dust jacket to wind up on the wall of Augustus Hasson's office, you'll have to appeal to a wide range of buyers."

Softening his tone, Brad went on. "What I'm trying to do is give you a realistic view of the publishing business. Sometimes I think the entire industry is heading for a nervous breakdown. Our self-image is enormously conflicted and confused. The internal battle between editorial and marketing is painful. But we have a job to do, and it requires turning opinion into fact—to move from an editor and a few marketing people saying, 'I like *The Mariah Project*,' to the public proclaiming, 'This is a good book.' To do that, we need a salable cover. So let me talk to our art director about lightening Carolyn Hewitt's hair. And, in the meantime, don't feel as though you're alone as a victim. Just last year, our art department screwed up and put the Acropolis on the dust jacket of a book about ancient Rome.''

That night, I cooked dinner for Big Walter and Patricia in what was billed as a farewell banquet before Patricia's departure for Italy.

''I'm not surprised,'' Big Walter said when I reported the jacket controversy. ''Nothing a publisher does surprises me.''

''The cover isn't that bad, really.''

''It's your book, goddamn it. Why don't you raise hell?''

Supressing the thought he might be right, I turned to Patricia. ''Are you excited about Italy?''

''Yes and no.''

''Why no?''

''I'll miss Big Walter.''

''Arrg-h-h,'' came the groan from her loving husband. ''The trip of a lifetime, and already she's ruining it. Actually,'' he added, looking toward me, ''what she's really worried about is the possibility I'll leave crumbs on the kitchen counter—or use her pots and pans. We have his-and-hers kitchen untensils. You didn't know that, did you?''

Drawing close, Patricia gave him an affectionate hug. ''I'm worried about you. That's all.''

''What's to worry? I might not know how to make boeuf bourguignon, but I can sauté chicken liver. And besides, having a jar of crunchy peanut butter in the kitchen is as important as being a good cook.''

Rolling her eyes, Patricia looked toward me. ''Tom, take good care of Big Walter while I'm gone, please.''

''I will, I promise.''

"Write it down," Big Walter exhorted. "Come on! Write it down on a piece of yellow paper so you don't forget."

The following morning, at 9:00, Patricia left. Big Walter and I brought her to the airport and waited in the Alitalia lounge until the plane departed. Then we went home, where I was eating lunch when Brad Carlisle called.

"I've just talked with an editor at *Horizon* magazine," he reported with considerable excitement. "They're interested in having you write an article on deep-sea mining for their October issue."

Laying aside my liverwurst sandwich, I asked the obvious questions: "How many words and how much money?"

"I don't know, but the magazine has five hundred thousand readers. It's aimed at a well-educated book-buying audience, and the article will carry a short note identifying you as the author of *The Mariah Project*. If one percent of those readers buys your book, that's five thousand copies."

"Does it really work like that?"

"It can't hurt. Look, Tom; the editor's name is Clara Jackson. I told her you'd call as soon as possible. Step number one in launching a best seller is an in-house swell, but after that you need help."

Appropriately primed, I bade Brad farewell and telephoned Clara Jackson. "It's an interesting topic," she acknowledged once I'd introduced myself. "We like slightly offbeat subjects, and, from what Brad tells me, this is an important area." For about five minutes, we discussed the magazine in general and the type of article Ms. Jackson wanted in particular. "Three thousand words is about right," she told me. "Our standard payment is twelve hundred dollars on acceptance, with a kill fee of two hundred."

"What do you mean, a kill fee of two hundred?"

"Oh, well, that's nothing to worry about. Occasionally, an

article comes in that's badly written, and we can't use it. When that happens, the author is free to sell it someplace else, and we pay a kill fee of two hundred dollars.''

"How often does that happen?''

"Hardly ever.''

"Who's the judge?''

"We are, of course. But, as I said, there's nothing to worry about. It rarely happens.''

Running her assurance through my mind, I detected a warning note.

"That's not enough. If the article's killed, I want four hundred dollars.''

"What?''

"This article will take me a week to write. If it's killed, which you seem to think won't happen, I want it to have been worth my while.''

Long pause . . . which became a gap.

"All right,'' she said at last. "It's highly unusual, but if the article is rejected, we'll pay four hundred dollars.''

That afternoon, congratulating myself on my negotiating talent, I went to work. Drawing largely on research from *The Mariah Project,* I began with a description of cobalt and manganese nodules discovered recently on the floor of the Atlantic:

The nodules build around organic material such as tiny fishbones, plant seeds, and teeth. They've grown in layers similar to tree rings at a rate of several millimeters per million years.

We have the technology to bring these nodules to the surface. Once there, they can be transferred to bulk carriers and transported to land-based processing plants.

*   *   *

At 7:00 P.M., I quit work and went over to Big Walter's to fulfill the vow of safekeeping I'd made to Patricia.

"The toaster's broken," he announced solemnly on my arrival. "Patricia's been gone for less than twelve hours, and already nothing works."

"No problem. If you want toast, we'll take a piece of bread and iron it."

"Very funny. I miss her so much, I can't even eat."

Serious problems lay ahead.

"Look, Big Walter. I know you're wallowing in an orgy of self-pity, but I'm hungry. So why don't you keep me company while I eat."

Weighing the request, he nodded assent.

"And since it's highly unlikely that you'll go the next ten days without eating, why don't you join me?"

Again the nod, this time more quickly.

"Atta boy! What's in the refrigerator?"

"Lots of stuff. Patricia went shopping before she left."

As promised, the refrigerator was exceedingly well stocked: cheese, cold cuts, some recently fried chicken.

"Doesn't Patricia tell you not to stand in front of the refrigerator with the door open?" I asked as Big Walter stood in front of the refrigerator with the door open.

"The food won't spoil in twenty seconds."

"You're evading the question. Doesn't she tell you to make up your mind with the door shut?"

In due course, we settled on the chicken.

"This is delicious," I complimented.

"Thank you. I found it on the subway last night. Just joking," he added.

To go with the chicken, we settled on a six-pack of Heineken. Midway through beer number two, Big Walter's spirits had brightened noticeably. "I finished my article, 'Why I Hate Computer Video Games,' " he told me.

"What'd you do with it?"

"Sent it to *New York* magazine with a letter saying I'd met Rupert Murdoch at a party and he wanted first look."

"What are your chances of their falling for that crap?"

"Fifty-fifty, maybe a little less."

As usual, our conversation covered a wide range of subjects.

"Patricia and I had a great honeymoon," Big Walter reminisced. "We went on a cruise in the Greek Islands, and there was this one man on board ship who fought with everybody. For two weeks, all he did was complain and argue. Without exception, he made everyone sick. Finally, the last day, I asked him what he did for a living, and he told me he was a psychiatrist."

"You're kidding!"

"No, I'm not, but it was a great trip. Swimming in the Mediterranean was fantastic. I got a really neat underwater mask, some fins, a snorkel, and an ear infection. That's what happens when you go around pretending you're a fish."

Around the time the chicken was gone, we switched topics: to politics, publishing, then to Laura, and finally back to Patricia.

"There's a very special way you can get to know someone," Big walter told me. "And, if you're lucky, it leads to a feeling that goes far beyond knowing, liking, respecting, and admiring. It's called love. In the eight years Patricia and I have been together, I've never once regretted being married."

"Do you ever miss being with other women?"

Taking his time, Big Walter answered. "Not really. Every now and then, I'll look at someone else and wonder what it would be like. But the truth is, I love Patricia so much, I can't imagine being with anyone else, not even for a night. I waited for our wedding the way a child waits for Christmas. You asked me once how I kept going, what keeps me alive through failure after screenwriting failure. It's all Patricia. I couldn't stand it without her. Sometimes at night I'll wake up and Patricia will be sleeping. I won't want to wake her, so I'll lie there perfectly still, not even moving. And I say to myself, 'God, I'm lucky.' The nicest thing that happens in my life is, at least once a day for no particular reason, she tells me she loves me. This is the first time we've been apart since before we were married, and, more than missing her, I feel guilty about not being able to give her trips to Europe and everything else she deserves. Someday, though, I'll make it up to her. I promise myself that every night.''

''Big Walter, I'm going to tell you something and I mean it. I don't know what standards the rest of the world goes by. But, as far as I'm concerned, Patricia already has an awfully good package. And, believe me, she knows it.''

July moved on in expected fashion. Big Walter continued his superintendent's duties and managed to make do in Patricia's absence. A food critic for the *Daily News* put tomatoes in his salad one night and liked them, so the next day he wrote an article about how tomatoes had made a remarkable comeback and were now ''in.'' *Harper's* magazine ran an article entitled ''In Praise of Books'' by Augustus Hasson. More appropriately, it should have been titled, ''In Praise of Augustus Hasson'' by Augustus Hasson. One thing he said, though, stayed with me:

Publishers are frightened by the thought of future technology. In ten years, the average consumer will be able to choose from a hundred TV programs simply by pushing a button. But books will endure, as they have throughout the ages. For anyone with an inquiring mind and the gift of imagination, there is no substitute for the printed word.

Ten days after her departure for Italy, Patricia came home. "I would have stayed longer," she announced at the airport, "but I assumed no one was vacuuming the apartment, and someone had to go marketing for Big Walter."

"Insults," he grumbled. "But what can you expect from a woman who eats her toast with a knife and fork."

That evening, a "welcome home" dinner in Patricia's honor was cooked by Patricia. "I missed you, you big dummy," she told Big Walter at the meal's end.

"Is it absolutely essential for you to refer to me as a big dummy?"

"What can I say? It fits."

Later in the week, I finished my article on deep-sea mining and mailed a copy to Clara Jackson at *Horizon* magazine. Then I took several days off to read *Crime and Punishment* and *The Brothers Karamazov*. Once or twice, Brad Carlisle called on minor matters. "You'll be pleased to know," he announced during one conversation, "last night at a cocktail party, an editor from Doubleday told me he'd heard *The Mariah Project* was first-rate."

"So how come Doubleday didn't make an offer at the auction?"

"I couldn't tell you. What matters, though, is that people who've never read the book are saying it's good. When that happens, the world is golden. By the way," he added. "I talked to our art department, and it's too late to lighten Carolyn Hewitt's hair on the dust jacket. The mechanicals are done, and, at this stage, any change would cost us several hundred dollars. Sorry!"

That afternoon, as a form of penance, a copy of the Wallace Press catalog for autumn arrived by messenger. Turning the pages, I came to the entry for *The Mariah Project*:

*   *   *

October 1st
$14.95
310 pages
Fiction

As captivating as any Ken Follett or John LeCarré
novel, *The Mariah Project* has created widespread in-
house enthusiasm. Played out on a global scale, the
drama involves . . .

Three paragraphs of hype followed, closing with the words,
"Thomas Hammond lives in Manhattan. This is his first
novel." Somewhat mollified, I brought the catalog to a local
Xerox shop and made copies for Big Walter and Laura. Then
I went back to the library to continue work on my textbook
revisions for Columbia University Press. The next few days
passed without incident, save for a remarkable event, which
occurred when Big Walter and I were jogging in the park.
Lying on the path directly in front of us was a twenty-dollar
bill. Big Walter saw it first, bent over, and picked it up.
Then, in what ranks among the more extraordinary acts I've
ever witnessed, he looked around to see if anyone in sight
appeared to be searching for lost money. He actually tried to
find the owner. "I don't know," he said later, when I asked
how anyone could be that honest. "I guess I felt bad for the
person who lost it."

   By the end of July, the textbook was complete. Satisfied
with the result and pleased it was finished, I started thinking
in terms of a new novel. Big Walter's article, "Why I Hate
Computer Video Games" was returned with a snotty note
from *New York* magazine. "No problem," he assured me. "I'll
submit it to the Op Ed page of *The New York Times* with a
letter of recommendation from A. O. Sulzberger."

Brad Carlisle reported that bound galleys on *The Mariah Project* had been sent to a number of reviewers. Judy Folger, the Wallace Press director of subsidiary rights, concluded that, unfortunately, the major book clubs weren't interested. Laura and I drove to York Harbor in southern Maine for a four-day weekend.

"Once upon a time, Augustus had a summer house near here," she reported after we'd found accommodations at an oceanside lodge. "It was in Cape Neddick, but he gave it up because long weekends interfered with his work."

"Doesn't that strike you as sadly compulsive?"

"Not really. He's made his life, and it keeps him happy."

Leaving the inn, we walked south along the shore. The afternoon sun was bright overhead, glistening on slick rocks and water.

"If you ask me, Augustus Hasson has all the charm of a magazine form letter soliciting a subscription renewal."

"If that's how you feel, why not change agents?"

Temporarily silenced, I groped for something to say in response. "Why is it that you're always so protective of Augustus?"

"I feel sorry for him. That's all."

"Why?"

"I'm not sure that's a proper subject for conversation." Looking out over the ocean, she seemed torn. "I'm not trying to be catty. It's just, my father told me something about him in confidence a long time ago, and, outside of Allen, I've never told anyone."

"It's up to you. If you can't tell me, I'll understand."

"That's what I like about you," she said with a smile. "You know when to tread softly instead of using a club. If I tell, you have to promise not to repeat it to anyone; not even Big Walter."

"Scout's honor."

Still gazing toward the ocean, Laura took my hand. "About thirty years ago, when Augustus was just out of college, he had an affair with a young woman of considerable social standing. She got pregnant and insisted on having the child. My father did some legal work on the matter."

"What did he do—help Augustus get out of paying child support?"

"To the contrary. The woman's family was quite wealthy. They didn't want money, and, even if they had, Augustus had nothing to give them. He sued for custody of the child."

"What!"

"You heard me. He sued for custody. It was quite revolutionary—at least thirty years ahead of its time. My father handled the case without a fee because Augustus didn't have the money to pay him. They lost, of course. Then the woman moved to California, and Augustus never saw her or the child again. He never married, and, to my knowledge, he hasn't spoken a word about the incident to my father or anyone else since then."

Late in the afternoon, the sky clouded over and we went back to our room. Laura seemed a bit remote; nothing I could put my finger on, but the distance was there. After dinner, we went back to the rocks along the shore. A full moon was visible through gaps in the clouds. We walked holding hands, listening to the ocean's roar.

"It's strange," Laura said, breaking the silence between us. "This is the first time in eight years I've been away with another man."

"And?"

"I don't know. I remember the first time I went away with Allen. About a month after we met, he suggested we go to Vermont for a long weekend. I'd never done that so soon with a man before. We weren't going for the trip. It was for the sake of being together alone. The first day was horribly hot and humid; we spent most of it on the front porch of our cabin. Then, in late afternoon, a huge storm broke, and the combination of dusk and heavy clouds made it seem like night. It was pouring rain with lightning and thunder. Everything smelled fresh and clean, and the only colors were green grass and green trees against a dark gray sky. . . . I'm sorry,'' she said, turning toward me. "I shouldn't——''

"It's all right," I said softly. "I understand."

"Do you?"

"I think so. . . . Why did you leave Allen?"

Drawing closer than she had before, Laura tightened her grip on my hand. "The marriage went sour. First it was little things. Then fights over concepts like mutual respect and sharing. Finally I realized I had to get drunk to enjoy sex with my husband. Allen used to tell me I wasn't his first sexual experience, but that he certainly hoped I'd be his last. After a while, I stopped wanting to go to bed with him."

"And then?"

"I got angry. I started to hate him for all of his shortcomings as well as mine. He was the prize I'd won and didn't want. Now the anger's gone. I just feel empty about the whole thing. Sometimes I think that, if I'd allowed myself an affair early on in the marriage instead of trying to be faithful, the resentment and tension wouldn't have built the way they did. We might have had a different relationship. But then again, maybe there's always a cloud."

I stood still, not knowing what to say, assaulted by memories of a time long gone.

"Tom, tell me I did the right thing by leaving. Sometimes I miss him."

18

ALL THINGS CONSIDERED, it wasn't a particularly comfortable weekend. The weather was good and both of us tried, but Laura's mind was somewhere else.

"I'm sorry," she said as we made our way down Route 95 toward New York. "I'm sure you've had better company in your life."

"Do you want to talk about it?"

"I suppose; not that it matters." Playing for time, she ran her hand along the edge of the glove compartment. "Last week I got a letter from Allen. Most of it he's told me a hundred times before—he loves me, he's miserable. But this time, there was a degree of self-insight and one or two negative comments about me that weren't entirely unfounded."

"Such as?"

"That I always concentrated on what was wrong with the marriage instead of building on what was right; that I can be

184

exceedingly stubborn and uncompromising; that the best times in the relationship were early on, when I put aside my doubts and focused on what we had. It's funny—the last few years I was always finding fault with Allen; always picking on him, and he never picked back. I remember, he told me once that either I was perfect or he was very tolerant. Now, looking back, I feel an enormous sense of loss, like a death. I guess losing someone you care about hurts. And on some level, despite everything, I still care about Allen.''

"You have to let go."

"I know, but I'm not as strong as you think I am. Everyone has experiences in life that cause pain. For some people, it's early childhood. For others, it's adolescence. Mine is now." Befitting the moment, Laura flashed one of her more rueful smiles. "Hey, Tom. I'm sorry. I apologize for ruining the weekend."

Back in Manhattan, I read, wrote, spent time with Big Walter, and baked an apple pie. Brad Carlisle called to report that *Publishers Weekly* had given *The Mariah Project* an excellent review, which would help considerably with prepublication orders. "Sometime this week, I'll mail you a copy," he promised.

Patricia and I spent a day museum-hopping while Big Walter stayed home to write. "When I was seven," Patricia confided, "an old woman with wrinkled skin and a cracked voice stopped me on the street when I was walking with my brother and told us, 'Someday you'll be as old as I am.' For years after that, I was afraid of growing old."

"When I was five," I added to the conversation, "I used to peel grapes because I wanted to see how they worked on the inside."

Late in the afternoon, we sat chewing blades of onion

grass on the lawn by The Cloisters. The sun was hot, moderated by a breeze blowing east off the Hudson River.

"How are things going with Laura?" Patricia queried.

"I'm not sure," I admitted. "Sometimes I feel like there's real closeness between us. Other times, we seem to be just going through the motions." The blade of grass I'd been chewing on was getting dehydrated, and I reached for another. "I keep trying to get close to Laura, and it seems as though half the time she's trying to pull away. One week she'll be too busy to get together; the next, everything is fine between us. Sometimes I feel as though Allen is still a factor; then things change, and it's hard to believe he ever even existed. I like Laura—I like her a lot. But sometimes I feel like I'm building on sand."

Patricia leaned back, shifting her weight to her elbow and side. "It's never easy, getting started as a couple. One of the things Big Walter taught me is, trust and affection don't come simply because you like someone or because a person is good-looking or bright. You earn them through hard work and lots of caring." Her eyes took on a slightly distant look, reaching back to a comfortable moment passed. "I remember when Big Walter and I started living together. Consolidating apartments is a great way to get to know someone. Every piece of furniture, every kitchen utensil, every ashtray and vase has a story—who gave it to you, what you were doing when it came into your life. Big Walter had four boxes of Kleenex and no toilet paper; two boxes of dishwasher detergent and no bathroom soap. By the time we finished unpacking, it was after midnight. We washed up and went to bed. Big Walter just lay there, staring at the ceiling. I asked what he was thinking about, and he told me, 'The apple crumb cake in the refrigerator.' "

"You're kidding!"

"No, I'm not. And then he told me he was happier than

he'd ever been in his life and he loved me. That was when I realized there were two kinds of people in the world. Big Walter and all the others. All my life, I'd been pursuing a fantasy; I guess we all are. But Big Walter is better than any fantasy I ever had." Patricia's smile vanished and was replaced by a slightly pensive look. "Tom, I want to ask you something. Do you think Big Walter will make it as a writer?"

"If there's a God in heaven, yes."

"And what if there isn't?"

"Then the devil will help him."

That night, I made dinner for Big Walter, Patricia, and Laura. You can't pick happiness off a tree, we decided. But each of us was working toward it as best we could.

Two days later, a heavy manila envelope bearing the latest issue of *Publishers Weekly* arrived in the mail from Wallace Press. Opening it up, I took note of Brad Carlisle's handwritten "congratulations" scrawled across the cover, then began turning pages. There was a brief news item about Random House's having accidentally remaindered every copy of a young author's first novel before publication because a computer error placed it on the wrong list. A short essay praised the portability of books as opposed to videocassette recorders and television sets. Mostly, though, the magazine consisted of advertisements aimed at booksellers. "The most torrid love affair since Antony and Cleopatra," read one notice:

And 50,000,000 book buyers will know about it in a six-figure promotion and ad campaign

- Sensuous foiled die-cut cover
- Forty-eight-copy floor display with special header
- $150,000 ad budget

- No other novel you will sell this year has the profit potential of this inevitable best seller.

"So this is how the publishing industry sells books," I said to myself.

Finally, I came to the review section, and honed in on the item I wanted:

THE MARIAH PROJECT
Thomas Hammond; Wallace Press, $14.95
ISBN 0-318-37263-6

In this well-crafted first novel, author Thomas Hammond tells the tale of a treasure hunt with global implications. CIA agent David Barrett is on the track of an energy source that could reshape the world. For help, he turns to a particularly enchanting heroine—the anatomically spectacular Carolyn Hewitt. Soon Israeli intelligence operatives, PLO terrorists, and countless others are drawn into the drama. *The Mariah Project* is a fast-paced thriller that excites and enthralls as it builds to a tension-packed climax. *6,000 first printing* (October 1).

The last line caught my eye: "*6,000 first printing*." Reaching for the phone, I dialed Brad's number. On the second ring, a secretary answered.

"This is Tom Hammond. Is he there?"

"I'm sorry, Mr. Hammond. Mr. Carlisle is on another line. Could I take your number and have him call you back."

"I'd rather hold."

Two minutes passed. Then a third. Finally, Brad came on. "Hi! What can I do for you?"

I thanked him for the magazine. Then: "But, Brad, there's something I don't understand. At the end, it says there's a first printing of six thousand. You told me it was twenty."

Long pause.

"Gee, I'm sorry. I thought I'd told you about the change. We'd planned on twenty, but, so far, orders have been sluggish. Most bookstores are reluctant to stock more than one or two copies of a first novel, and the jobbers are ambivalent."

"What's a jobber?"

"That's hard to describe exactly. Basically, they're in the order-fulfillment business. They read books, buy in large lots, and distribute titles to small stores. If the jobbers don't buy a book and the big stores don't pick it up on their own, there's no point in a first run of twenty thousand."

"I don't understand. How many bookstores are there in the United States?"

"Tom, that's irrelevant. There's no way we can force stores to stock a given book, and the most expensive thing in the world is overprinting. Besides, even if we could force books into the marketplace, they'd just come back. Alfred Knopf said it best: gone today, here tomorrow."

"Very clever. Look, Brad——"

"I'm sorry," he said, moderating his tone. "I don't mean to be flippant. And, believe me, I have faith in the book. But these things start slowly. So far, orders on *The Mariah Project* are running at twenty-eight hundred. We're still in the process of establishing a market. *Publishers Weekly* should help; so will your *Horizon* article. The other thing I've done is given several copies of the galleys to our publicity department. The woman in charge is Wendy Schultz. Give her a call, and see what she can set up for you."

My next call went to Wendy Schultz, who expressed delight at the sound of my voice but was booked up for most of the week. Checking her appointment calendar, she suggested we meet on Friday at 3:00. Then I telephoned Clara Jackson at *Horizon* magazine to find out when my article on deep-sea mining would be published.

"Sorry I haven't gotten back to you," Clara said. "The article is good, but it needs some revision."

"Like what?"

"Somehow you have to make it livelier; add a little sex appeal, if you will. The way it reads now is too scientific and flat. You have to do something to make it more dramatic."

Off the record, I thought she was full of crap. The article seemed fine to me the way it was. Still, books belong to the author, magazine articles to the editor. Ergo, a rewrite was in order. Resorting to the trusty Hammond Index-Card Method, that afternoon I began to take notes:

> If all the gold that has been mined from the beginning of time were consolidated, it would form a single cube with eighteen-yard sides. Yet a massive underseas find could reduce the value of gold below that of silver.

> One danger inherent in deep-sea mining is that spores, bacteria, and other noxious creatures dormant on the ocean floor for millions of years might flourish unchecked if brought to the surface.

By Friday at noon, a "sexy rewrite" that spoke of raising manganese nodules through "miles of cold, dark, treacherous water" was in the mail. Then I went down to Wallace Press to meet Wendy Schultz. "I'm *so* glad you could come," she gushed when we shook hands in the reception area. "Brad is enormously excited about your book." Jabbering away about what a shame it was we hadn't gotten a book-club offer, she led me to her office. Piles of paper were stacked on the windowsill. A dying plant, brown at the edges, drooped by her desk. A single shelf, jammed with copies of the latest

Wallace Press releases, ran the length of the far wall. Ms. Schultz herself was slobby and overweight, about forty with wiry brown hair piled up over her head like a New Year's Eve party noisemaker and a gravy stain on her blouse. Judging from the way she kept her office, it was a fifty-fifty proposition as to whether she'd put the blouse on dirty to begin with or spilled something at lunch.

"Unfortunately, Mr. Hammond, the big TV shows are beyond our reach. Nothing sells books like Phil Donahue or Johnny Carson, but they're interested only in name authors. The same is true of Merv Griffin and Dick Cavett, so, for the time being, we're concentrating on radio. I'm sure many people will be interested in a novel about undersea oil.''

"Crystals,'' I corrected.

"Pardon?''

"The discovery was a mother lode of energy-producing crystals.''

"Oh, yes, of course. Anyway, we'll be contacting local radio stations shortly. Meanwhile, copies of the book have been sent to a number of reviewers, including *The New York Times*. That's the important one. A good review in the *Times* would be just marvelous. All we can do is hope they're interested in a story about—what was it you said was in the ocean again?''

"Crystals. Energy-producing crystals. Ms. Schultz, let me ask you something. You're the PR person assigned to my book. Have you read it?''

Momentarily flustered, my "promo expert'' ran a finger along the gravy stain on her blouse. "Well, no. But, of course, I understand it's quite good. You see, with all the books we publish, well, the publicity department is understaffed, so it's impossible for us to read everything.''

"Do me a favor. Read my book.''

"Well, yes. I suppose I could. And, of course, as soon as

we get reviews from *Kirkus* and *Library Journal,* I'll see that Mr. Carlisle sends them to you.''

"Thank you."

Regaining the composure she'd lost when I began my mini-assault, Ms. Schultz's face assumed proportions midway between vacuous and stupid. "Well, yes. Now there is one other matter to discuss. Sometimes, to help launch a new book, we ask the author to provide us with names and addresses. If you'll be so kind as to take a hundred-or-so envelopes and address them to family members and friends, we'll mail them out with an announcement just before publication date. That way, people will go into stores and ask for your book. It increases orders and will make booksellers more aware of your work."

Taking a box of two hundred Wallace Press envelopes, I left and went back to my apartment. For about an hour, I considered calling Brad Carlisle to get a more precise fix on what was happening to my novel. Then I decided maybe I was blowing things out of proportion. And anyway, Big Walter would be more sympathetic.

"She sounds like an ass," he noted cheerfully after I'd presented a rundown of the day's events.

"That's putting it mildly. From what I saw today, Wendy Schultz has the organizational ability of an untrained gerbil."

"So what comes next?"

"I don't know. But *The Mariah Project* is my livelihood. Whether or not I eat well this year depends on how much I earn from writing, and what's happening at Wallace Press doesn't exactly inspire confidence. The first printing was cut from twenty thousand to six. The PR person assigned hasn't even read the book. Store orders are next-to-nothing. The dust jacket is mediocre. Big Walter, I'm worried."

For a good ten seconds, Big Walter was silent.

"All right," he finally said. "Look at the bright side. The

only review you have so far is fantastic. Your agent is one of the most powerful men in publishing, with his own pipeline to the media. The book doesn't come out until October first. There's no way you can realistically expect anything yet. The world at large still thinks you're a professor. Give it a chance."

Frustration. Hope. Maybe Big Walter was right.

"Big Walter, what are you doing this weekend?"

"Why?"

"Because I need your help addressing envelopes."

So we addressed envelopes. Saturday morning, Big Walter and I sat down and made up a list of virtually everyone we knew. After a while, the job got a bit tedious, but the cause was good.

"I addressed one with your name on it," Big Walter announced midway through the project. "That's because you're my good friend, and I know you like letters."

"Thank you. I did one for you and Patricia an hour ago."

The following day, we went to Coney Island with Patricia and Laura. "Look at that ocean," Big Walter murmured, gazing out at the Atlantic. "Every time I see the waves and tide, I can't help but think of manganese nodules."

On Monday I called Clara Jackson at *Horizon* magazine to see if she'd gotten my revisions, but she was away from her desk. Tuesday, when the call hadn't been returned, I tried again—with the same result. "Maybe I'm missing something," I told Big Walter that night. "But I can't understand why people don't have the basic courtesy to return telephone calls." Wednesday, I tried reaching Brad Carlisle, but the entire publishing industry seemed to have been away from its desk for a week.

"Editors don't work for a living," Big Walter advised when I sought solace. "They just annoy people. If William

Shakespeare submitted *Macbeth* to a modern-day publisher, they'd tell him to cut the sleepwalking scene as unrealistic. The idea of Lady Macbeth sticking her hand in the ocean and turning the water incarnadine would have driven them crazy.''

Brad called, finally. "*Library Journal* gave us a good review," he reported. "*Kirkus* was snotty, but, on the whole, positive.''

Clara Jackson failed to return a third call. At week's end, I learned why. "Dear Mr. Hammond," the letter read:

> Enclosed herewith is your article on deep-sea mining. Unfortunately, it's not right for *Horizon* magazine, but we certainly appreciate your giving us a look. Also enclosed is a check for your kill fee in the amount of two hundred dollars.
>
> Sincerely,
> *Clara Jackson*

Two hundred dollars. *Two hundred dollars*. The deal was *four* hundred! Red in the face, I picked up the telephone and dialed her number.

"I'm sorry," the secretary said. "Ms. Jackson is tied up at the moment.''

"Then untie her.''

"Really, she's quite busy.''

"I don't care. I want to talk to her now.''

Seconds later, I was disconnected.

Dial again.

"Look, I don't care if she's busy. I want to talk to her now, or my next call goes to the managing editor.''

Twenty seconds . . . Thirty . . .

"Hello, Tom. This is Clara. I'm terribly sorry, but *Smithsonian* magazine has an article on deep-sea mining this month, so the topic's passé.''

"And what about the kill fee?"

"We sent you a check for two hundred dollars."

"I know. The deal was four hundred."

Long pause.

"But Tom, that's not possible. Our standard kill fee is two hundred. Half the articles we commission are killed. We couldn't *possibly* pay each author four hundred dollars."

"Half the articles! You told me it almost never happened!"

"Well, it wouldn't have happened this time if you wrote better. The truth is, your article was rather boring. The audience for it would have been extremely limited."

"Look, lady. You owe me four hundred dollars."

"It's a pity, isn't it, Mr. Hammond, that there's nothing in writing to that effect. Good day."

"I'll kill her," I told Big Walter an hour later. "I'll take her neck and twist it around so many times she'll look like a pretzel."

"And then what?"

"I'll go to jail, and Norman Mailer will get me out because I'm a literary talent."

Nodding in acquiescence, Big Walter advanced his next thought. "Actually, Clara Jackson was right. It was a mistake not to get it in writing."

"Thank you. I'm glad you pointed that out because I've never made a mistake before. Without your telling me, I wouldn't have recognized it."

"All right, don't get touchy. If you're that mad, sue them."

"What!"

"Sue them. Go down to Small Claims Court, fill out a form, and sue them." Reaching for the Manhattan telephone directory, he thumbed through the pages under "New York City Government." "Here it is—Civil Court/Small Claims

Division, 111 Centre Street. . . . Turn it around; make them sweat.''

That afternoon, a little apprehensive about entering the court system, I took the subway to Chambers Street and walked east to a squat concrete building marked ''New York City Civil Court.'' Twenty-or-so people were milling around the lobby with no information desk in sight. A sign taped to the wall read ''Small Claims Court Office—Room 323.'' Following a series of arrows, I found the elevator and rode up. Room 323 was a small room with scuffed grey linoleum, dirty walls, and acoustic tiles above. A long counter manned by two middle-aged men was at one end. A grey metal table of World War II vintage stood in room-center with a pile of claim forms on top:

	CIVIL COURT——
CITY OF NEW YORK	MAXIMUM: $1,500
SMALL CLAIMS PART—TIME OF TRIAL: 6:30 pm	
REQUEST FOR INFORMATION	

CLAIM AGAINST:
(THEIR NAME AND ADDRESS)

CLAIM BY:
(YOUR NAME AND ADDRESS)

AMOUNT: $

STATE YOUR CLAIM HERE:

Filling out a form, I inserted a claim for $400, then got on line behind a young woman who took forever. Finally, I reached the counter. "That will be four dollars and fifty-five cents," the heavier of the two clerks said.

I paid, and he copied the information onto a second sheet of paper.

"Be here at six-thirty on September twelfth."

Then, still seething over the week's events, I left the office and made my way to the lobby, where I got the bright idea of calling Augustus Hasson. After all, he was my agent and would want to know if I sued someone. And, more to the point, maybe he could get *The Mariah Project* rolling. Locating a pay phone, I dialed The Great One's number.

"Mr. Hasson, please," I told the secretary who answered. "It's Tom Hammond calling."

As expected, I was put on hold.

"Hi, Tom. This is Marcia Steinberg. Is there anything I can do to help?"

"Actually, I was hoping to speak with Mr. Hasson."

"He's quite busy. What seems to be the problem?"

Beset by a mixture of resentment and resignation, I poured out what had happened: slow orders, a cut in the first printing, unanswered telephone calls, a PR person who didn't know the first thing about my novel.

For the first time ever, Marcia Steinberg sounded sympathetic. "All right," she told me. "I'll talk to Mr. Hasson as soon as he's available. But be patient, and try to remember, you have only one publisher and one book. We have a dozen of each every month."

Late in the afternoon, I arrived home and telephoned Big Walter.

"I can't talk," he told me. "The building boiler just sprung a leak, and I have to go down to the basement."

"That's okay. Everyone else in publishing is too busy to talk to me. Why should you be any different?"

"Tom," he said with magnanimity in his voice. "I'd love

to talk with you. So why don't you come over for a little chat? And, when you do, bring a mop because, at this very moment as we talk, the basement is flooding.''

Over the weekend, I sought another dose of sympathy—this one from Laura. Friday over dinner, then back at her apartment; Saturday, as we picnicked by the Palisades in New Jersey. For all the times I'd held her hand regarding Allen, I figured she owed me one. And, I must say, she was supportive. ''I understand what you're going through,'' she told me as we sat on the cliffs overlooking the river. ''In some ways, you and I are two of a kind. Everything's always come easy for us, so it's hard to deal with obstacles beyond our control.''

''But *The Mariah Project* is good. Everyone says so.''

''I know. But publishing is a funny business. The moment a house signs up a novel, it starts looking for ways to cut its losses. And salesmen get paid on a salary-commission basis, so there's not much incentive for them to hassle over two copies of *The Mariah Project* when it's just as easy to go into a store and sell forty copies of the latest book by Robert Ludlum.''

''But this is my book.''

''And forty thousand other authors with books due this year feel the same as you do. Tom, I'm not sure how to explain this, but have you ever heard of triage?''

''Sure—it's hospitals in wartime, or something like that.''

''All right. Try to think of publishing in terms of triage. During a battle, when medical resources are scarce, the wounded are divided into three categories. The first are soldiers who'll recover if treated promptly. They're given attention first. Then come those who might survive. They're treated if facilities are available. Finally, you have the wounded who are going to die no matter what's done for them. Except for painkillers, they get no medical treatment at all. Publishers operate in a surprisingly similar manner. There's not a lot in the way of available resources, so healthy writers get most of the attention. Sometimes the system works nicely, and quality writers like William Styron and Saul Bellow rise to the top. Every now and then, a book left for dead turns out to be a survivor. I don't know where *The Mariah Project* fits into the spectrum, but . . ." Her voice trailed off, then picked up again. "Tom, when a general sends troops into battle, he knows some of them will die. And, depending on attack plans and battle formations, he even has a pretty good idea of which ones. But he doesn't tell them."

Knowing she was right, and coming to grips with the week just done, I sat silent.

"Where did you learn so much about publishing?" I asked at last.

"It's genetic. I was born smart."

"You know something? Someday I might want to marry you."

Suddenly rigid, Laura pulled back. "Don't say that."

"Why not?"

"Because I don't want you to. Please! Just don't." Then her voice softened. "Tom, this is a difficult time for me. Maybe I'm making the same mistakes all over again by putting up too many barriers between us; maybe not. But right now, you have the strength and inner resources to sustain a relationship. I don't."

19

THE LAST DAYS of August were a time of hope. Brad Carlisle called to report that Waldenbooks had ordered 400 copies of *The Mariah Project*. Alex and Edna Kramer (who owned the neighborhood bookstore) stopped me on the street to say they'd ordered six. Augustus Hasson sent a short note promising to do his best to place a gossip item in the *New York Post*.

"That's the least he can do," Big Walter grumbled. "He's your agent. He works for you."

"KBI (keep believing it)," I answered.

Meanwhile, Laura reported with a degree of ambivalence that Allen had begun dating another woman.

"How does that make you feel?" I queried.

"A little relieved, a little jealous."

"Do you think it's serious?"

"I don't know. But if it is, I apologize in advance for all the problems this blow to my ego will cause you."

"No need," I told her. "I've gotten a lot of sustenance and emotional support from you."

"Have you really?"

Matching her smile as best I could, I nodded.

"Tom, you've helped me over so many hurdles. I hope you understand how much I care about you."

One week before Labor Day, classes resumed at Fordham. Finishing up some odds and ends, I spent several days in the library, lunching once with Sylvia Pennock. Big Walter decided to try his hand at a short story—about a building superintendent who falls in love with a lady mud wrestler. Leonard Macy (the managing editor of *Horizon* magazine) telephoned to ask whether I really thought I could gain anything by suing.

"I already have," I told him. "Just filling out the complaint form was enormously satisfying."

For several minutes, we discussed my claim that Clara Jackson had promised a kill fee of $400. "I'm sorry," Macy said at the close of our conversation. "Clara tells me it was two hundred, and I have to believe my editor."

Later that day, I sought out Sylvia Pennock. "Hey, Sylvia. Do you know anything about Small Claims Court?"

"A little. One of our professors took the class there last winter."

"How would you like to be my lawyer?"

"Neat, really neat."

That night, Big Walter agreed to serve as chief character witness.

"That's highly appropriate," Patricia noted, "because there's no doubt whatsoever that Big Walter is a character."

Growing more captivated by the prospect of battle, I even

considered subpoenaing Augustus Hasson to testify as to my literary talent. Somehow, though, I didn't think The Great One would appreciate a subpoena. And I doubted very much that he'd testify without one.

September began with a rush of cool weather. With all my "make-work" projects complete, I began active consideration of a second novel. *New York* magazine ran a profile on the editor of *The New York Times Book Review*, describing him as "the most powerful individual in all of publishing" . . . "The *Times Book Review* might not be successful in telling people what to think," the article concluded, "but it's remarkably successful in telling its readers which books they should buy and think about."

Of particular note was the process by which books sent to the *Times* were chosen for deification:

> The *Times Book Review* receives forty thousand books a year. Seven preview editors skim one hundred books per person per week and make recommendations at a weekly editorial meeting. The entire staff contributes to a final decision. The odds of a book being chosen are one in forty.

One in forty! It was a slim thread to hang my hopes from. Still, if the fates were willing, it would come to fruition.

Another week passed. A publication called *Booklist* ran a favorable review of *The Mariah Project*. Laura went up to Connecticut to spend several days with her parents. Big Walter called an official halt to his long-forgotten diet. "What can I say," he admitted. "I just happen to be one of those people who think fasting means not eating dessert."

Two days before Labor Day weekend, I received a telephone call from Brad Carlisle.

"They're in," he announced.

"What's in?"

"Finished books; your novel. Come on over and I'll give you a copy."

I would have taken a cab, but, midtown traffic being what it is, the subway was faster. Even so, the half hour it took to get to Wallace Press seemed forever. Another eternity, which must have lasted two minutes, passed while I waited in the reception area until Brad appeared and led me to his office.

"There it is," he said, pointing to a copy of *The Mariah Project* on the edge of his desk. "Congratulations!"

Transfixed, I picked up the book—and stared. I'm not quite sure how to explain this, but seeing and holding *The Mariah Project* was one of the most exciting moments of my life. It was a real honest-to-goodness book! Not 300 pages of typed copy that might someday be published; not some article I'd written for my high school newspaper. It was a genuine, printed, the-kind-you-buy-in-stores book—with my photograph on the dust jacket. Suddenly, all the hassles of the past sixteen months seemed worthwhile.

"I hope you're happy with it," Brad said. "It's a nice type size and design layout."

Peeling back the dust jacket, I looked at the cover—charcoal gray with red binding. Even the binding was nice. "It's great," I whispered. "I think it's fantastic."

"I'm glad you like it. Sometimes production screws up and prints a book upside-down or with the cover backwards. This one came off the presses without a mistake."

I held my copy, turning pages as we talked. The title page; a copyright notice; my own Library of Congress catalog number.

"I haven't had time to call Augustus," Brad said. "Usually he asks us to send him a copy. I can do it, or you can bring it over yourself. It wouldn't hurt to show up in person at a moment of triumph."

I nodded, and Brad pointed to a plastic shopping bag on the floor by his desk. "Under the contract, you're entitled to six books. I put them in there along with a few extras. The bag is from Gristede's. You can keep it."

Marcia Steinberg answered the front door when I arrived at The Augustus Hasson Literary Agency. Obviously, she'd seen novels before and wasn't particularly impressed. "Oh, that's wonderful," she said, radiating an interest level that made me feel like a four-year-old showing off a sweet potato rooting in water. It occurred to me that, with a little more intelligence and larger breasts, she'd be perfectly cast as the evil bitch in a television soap opera.

"If it's all right, I'd like to give it to Mr. Hasson in person."

"He's very busy."

"I know, but it won't take long. Besides, I want to ask him something."

Shrugging in resignation, she turned and led me down the corridor to the reception area. The door to the inner office was open, and I could hear The Great One dictating letters to his secretary. "Sign those for me," he concluded. At a pause in the monologue, Ms. Steinberg slipped into the office, passing the secretary who was on her way out. Then the door closed, and I was left standing beneath the framed dust jacket of *Kennedy's Women*.

"Would you like a seat?" the secretary queried.

Before I could answer, Marcia Steinberg reappeared. "He'll see you now, Mr. Hammond."

Our ritual greeting was the same as ever: The Great One seated at his glass-topped desk, not bothering to stand up; my sitting in the chrome-armed chair opposite.

"I have a wonderful new author," Hasson said, deviating from the pattern long enough for a moment's small talk. "New to me, of course. He's had several previous publications. Yesterday morning, we signed a two-book contract with Doubleday for six hundred thousand dollars." Pausing so I could evaluate the enormity of his accomplishment, King Augustus straightened a thin sheaf of papers on his desk. "Now, what was it you wanted to talk about?"

Reaching into my plastic bag, I drew out a copy of *The Mariah Project*. "Brad Carlisle suggested I bring you this."

Just for a moment, Augustus Hasson seemed human. I'm not quite sure why or how, but I think it was his eyes, the way he looked at the book—with a mixture of pride, warmth, maybe even a touch of envy.

"That's wonderful," he said—the same words Marcia Steinberg had spoken moments earlier, but this time they had feeling. "Congratulations!"

Reaching across the desk, he offered his hand. I took it, and was surprised by the firmness of his grip. Then there was silence—an indication it was time to leave.

"There's one thing more, Mr. Hasson. I know you're busy, but I have a good friend named Walter Walker, who's a writer. I wondered if you'd be willing to read one of his screenplays and possibly represent him as his agent."

Looking as if he was about to brush away a nettlesome fly, The Great One leaned forward. "What's his publishing history?"

"So far, he's unpublished."

"Tom, I appreciate the offer; but, as I'm sure you're aware, I'm extremely busy. The only reason I took you on was because you're a friend of Laura Kinney's. . . . That, of course, plus the fact that you're a talented young writer."

"Yes, sir. I understand."

"Very well, then. Tell Mr. Walker I'm sorry, and give him my regards."

Big Walter was in the building lobby, mop in hand, when I arrived in jogging clothes an hour later.

"Give me five minutes," he said. "Then I'll race you the length of the park."

Taking a seat on the lobby's tiled steps, I began to offer words of support. "Bend over! Mop harder!"

Ignoring the exhortations (and the plastic shopping bag under my arm), he continued work at a steady methodical pace. Five minutes later, the floor was spotless.

"What's under your arm?" he asked at last.

"A present."

"For me, I hope."

Utilizing every dramatic gesture I could muster, I reached into the bag and drew out a copy of *The Mariah Project*.

"Oh, my God!" Big Walter murmured. "Can I touch it?"

"It's yours, to keep."

Gently, with tenderness and care appropriate for holding a five-day-old infant, he cradled the book. Then, one at a time, as I'd done a few hours earlier, he turned the pages. Library of Congress data; a copyright notice. Finally, the dedication, set in type just before the title page of the book:

> *For Big Walter,*
> *the best friend I ever had.*

"Look at that," Big Walter whispered. "Look at that!"

That night, under my door, there was a poem—which, in all its glory, read as follows:

*   *   *

I tried to write a poem for you
It's not an easy thing to do
But your dedication touched my heart
And with your book I'll never part
My pace and meter are real poor
In rhythm I will write no more
With every line this poem gets worse
I guess my gift is not for verse

Beneath the poem were the words:

Dear Tom,

If I look a little heavy these days, it's because I'm
bursting with pride.
Thank you.

With affection,
Big Walter

20

With September underway and *The Mariah Project* heading for bookstores across the country, a banner performance seemed remote but possible. I wanted the book to be a best seller. That might sound hypocritical after all the things I've said about epics like *Strawberries at Midnight*, but writing was my way of earning a living as well as my way of life. Financial gain plus a little recognition were natural objectives.

The first recognition was minute, at best: a one-paragraph letter from Augustus Hasson:

Dear Tom,

Let me congratulate you on *The Mariah Project*. In light of your achievement, I thought you might appreciate a copy of the enclosed photograph.

Attached to the letter was an autographed eight-by-ten glossy photo—of Augustus Hasson.

"What are you going to do with it?" Big Walter asked when I showed it to him that night.

"I don't know. I don't suppose you'd want it."

"You've got to be kidding." Suddenly his eyes began to glow. "Maybe we could hang it in the men's room of a gay bar with Hasson's telephone number underneath."

Just for a moment, I had visions of my next sojourn to The Great One's office: "Tom, in recent days I've received a number of very strange telephone calls. Having traced their origin to a certain photograph, and remembering a rather impetuous letter you once wrote to Richard Stoddart, I was wondering if——"

"Just joking," Big Walter added.

September progressed with omens that were good. Two days before my case against *Horizon* magazine was scheduled for trial, Leonard Macy telephoned with an offer to settle. "I'm not saying you're right," he began the negotiations, "but it's not worth our while to go to court over a few dollars. Why don't we split the difference and call it three hundred."

"Mr. Macy, you owe me four hundred dollars."

"I understand your position, Mr. Hammond. I'm offering to compromise."

"Four hundred dollars plus two subway tokens and another four dollars and fifty-five cents for the cost of the complaint."

"Mr. Hammond, taking a hard-line position will get you nowhere. I urge you to be reasonable!"

We settled on $390, which was pretty much what I'd wanted. Buoyed by the victory, I treated my attorney and chief character witness to lunch. Then, after shopping for some clothes and taking a few days off, I began work in earnest on The Second Great American Novel.

For some time, I'd wrestled with the idea of what to write next. Part of me leaned toward a sequel to *The Mariah Project,* which would keep David Barrett and Carolyn Hewitt alive. Another part said their story had already been told and it was time to concentrate on new creations. Tentatively, I'd settled on a second thriller—this one set in the mountains of Nepal. Like *The Mariah Project,* it had an overlay of CIA intrigue, but the focus was vastly different.

As I'd done sixteen months earlier, I began to research. The Columbia University library system had forty books on Nepal, and index cards returned to my life. Scraps of lined yellow paper soon became prevalent. All things considered, Hammond Opus No. 2 was off to a good start. As for Opus No. 1, there were problems.

"Orders have stalled at thirty-one hundred," Brad said one afternoon when I called his office. "At this point, we'll need help from the outside—book reviews and PR to get things rolling."

"What about ads?"

"We're going to wait a bit. There's no point in spending a lot of money until we see where it will do us the most good."

"What does that mean?" I pressed.

"It means we have no plans to advertise at present. But everyone here is keeping a close eye on the situation. At the first sign of light, believe me, we'll pounce."

Later that day (much to my amazement), Wendy Schultz called to report that she'd set up a radio interview for the October 1 publication date. "And do think positively, Mr. Hammond," she exhorted. "It's such a wonderful book. The parts I read were simply marvelous."

That evening, just before dusk, I went jogging with Big

Walter. "Not a penny for ads," I groused as we made our way along the promenade overlooking the river. "Not one single solitary cent."

"Cheer up. Patricia and I will listen to you on the radio."

"Didn't you hear what I just said? *Miss Piggy's Guide to Life* has an ad budget of a billion dollars. Garfield the Cat has full-page ads all over the place. How would you like to lose a literary competition to a pig and a cat?"

"I wouldn't like it."

"Sometimes, I think the entire publishing industry should be revamped. Best-selling books get the care and attention of a presidential election. Everything else is dumped on the market. How——"

"Hey, Tom."

"What is it?"

"I don't mean to cause trouble. But, over there, look!"

The promenade was pretty empty. Several joggers were on our side of the concrete runway. Two roller skaters and a solitary bike rider were directly ahead. And making her way between them, in all her glory, wearing a pale blue T-shirt and white shorts, was The Fantasy Jogger—with a guy beside her.

Involuntarily, I stopped dead in my tracks.

Her hair was an inch or two longer than I'd remembered; still kept in place by a terrycloth band. Everything else was unchanged. Her eyes, her smile, everything about her—it was Carolyn Hewitt. Talking as they ran, she and her companion swept by.

"Hey," Big Walter interrupted, breaking my trance. "Are you all right?"

The guy was five-nine, maybe an inch taller. He looked like a college professor.

"Tom, are you okay?"

"I'm fine," I mumbled, staring into the distance at the

vanishing figure. "It's just, once upon a time, I was in love with her."

Publication date came on October 1. The radio interview went nicely. *The Kansas City Star* ran a favorable book review; the *Dallas Times-Herald* one that wasn't so hot. Several days later, I received a long, rambling letter from a Dallas suburbanite. "Pay no attention to the *Times-Herald,*" he wrote. "Newspaper writers are Communist agitators." There followed a near-endless, mostly incoherent attack on the news media which closed with the claim that Walter Cronkite was a pawn of "the international Zionist conspiracy" and Dan Rather was "an Iranian poet."

Also in the mail was a congratulatory note from a former colleague at Columbia. "It wasn't easy to find your book," he reported. "Most of the stores I went to said they'd never heard of it."

Around noon, I made an anonymous tour of bookstores in midtown Manhattan. Scribner's and Coliseum had copies of *The Mariah Project.* Doubleday, Dalton, and Barnes & Noble didn't. "We're only interested in major books," the last salesperson I spoke with said; "not marginal novels."

"I've got an idea," Big Walter suggested when I filled him in over lunch. "Why don't we kill some landlords and leave copies of the book by each carcass. As the landlord toll mounts, you can't imagine how much publicity you'll get."

"Big Walter, that's an absolutely fantastic idea."

"Thank you. I thought you'd like it."

Wendy Schultz called that afternoon to report setting up a second interview: this one with WNYC radio. As usual, she appeared to be playing with a less-than-full deck. "By the way," I asked as the conversation progressed, "whatever happened to those envelopes I addressed?"

"Oh, my goodness! Mr. Hammond, I forgot all about

them. But, now that you've reminded me, I'll see to it that they're mailed out by the end of the week.''

Brad Carlisle was away from his desk when I called, and didn't call back. Two days later, the WNYC radio interview was canceled.

"And that's where things stand," I told Laura on Friday night. "It's one big disappointment after another."

"Cheer up," she said, "Martin Cruz Smith wrote thirty-eight novels before *Gorky Park*."

"What's cheerful about that? All it means is I'll have to go through this phenomenon thirty-seven more times before I get a best seller."

We walked as we talked; across 79th Street to pick up a copy of *The New York Times*; then down West End Avenue to my apartment. Inside, I hung our coats in the closet, and Laura reached for her purse.

"I've started smoking," she announced, taking out a cigarette.

"Since when?"

"It's an old habit. Allen used to bug me about it, so when we got married, I quit. . . . Now—it helps me cope. . . ."

Her voice drifted off.

Once again, the gap between us seemed to be widening. I wasn't sure what to say next.

"You've seemed awfully distant lately."

"I don't mean to be," Laura answered. "Actually, what you're witnessing is insecurity and self-doubt. I'm wrestling with problems that are terribly difficult, and sometimes I feel less than confident about the choices I've made."

"Do you still love him?"

There was a pause.

"Maybe."

"Why?"

"I don't know. Out of habit, I guess." Looking directly at

me, she forced a smile. "Tom, how do you know when you really love someone?"

"I don't know. I suppose you love someone when you care about making them happy."

Again the smile, very forced.

Reaching out, I rested a hand on her shoulder.

"Let's read the paper," Laura said.

The Saturday *Times* has two sections. I took the second, Laura the first. We read in silence, aware of each other's presence but not really sharing the moment. "If you're fighting to keep from getting involved," I wanted to say, "you're missing the point of this relationship." Then——

"Oh, my God!"

"What's the matter?"

"Oh, my God. Tom, look at this!"

Peering over her shoulder, I stared down at the Op Ed page of the one-and-only *New York Times*:

WHY I HATE COMPUTER VIDEO GAMES
By B. W. WALKER

Years ago, when I was in college, the student union housed an old jukebox that always seemed to be playing. The Beatles, The Fifth Dimension—I loved those songs.

Have you been to a student union lately? The campus jukebox is no more. It's been replaced by computer video games. Instead of Simon and Garfunkel, the sounds of rapid machine-gun fire (excuse me—galaxy-destruction vaporizer blasts) fill the air. The names most revered by students are no longer McCartney, Lennon, Harrison, and Ringo Starr—but Pac-Man, Galaxion, Tron, Stargate, Pole Position, Centipede, Asteroids, Asteroids Deluxe, Zoo Keeper, Robotron, Roc'n Rope and Donkey Kong.

Beep!
Splat!
Arrgh!

What I'm about to say might brand me as a 270-pound fuddy-dud. Others may liken my thoughts to the Luddites', who went about smashing machinery in nineteenth-century England. But here goes: *I hate computer video games.*

Why?

Let's put the matter in perspective. I grew up with chess, checkers, Monopoly and Scrabble—games that were social in nature. Computer buffs might argue that playing chess is inconsistent with extended conversation, but many a friendship has been solidified in quiet combat while pondering a knight to rook four. The games of my childhood were portable. At one time or another, most everyone in my generation played checkers outdoors in the midday sun. And the games were durable. My Monopoly and Scrabble sets are a quarter-century old and still in vintage working order. Even the simplest of old-fashioned toys was incredibly versatile. Give a plain wooden broom handle to a child and—presto—you had (1) a horse, (2) a limbo bar, or (3) a bat for stickball. Once I even smashed the neighborhood bully in the face with a broom handle.

By contrast, most video games are played alone. And even when two people play, they're too busy pushing buttons to talk. Prolonged exposure to computer video games leads to decreased attention spans in children. Video games require little in the way of creative thought, and authorized dealers charge standard fees of fifty dollars and up to repair broken computer game consoles.

But let's go back to chess for a moment. With devotees in every civilized land, it's the most universal of all games. A crude chessboard and pieces were found in King Tutankhamen's tomb. Terracotta pieces believed to be six thousand years old have been unearthed in Northern Iraq (formerly Mesopotamia). I doubt very much that Donkey Kong will be in vogue six thousand years from now. Nor will future generations wax nostalgic over beeps and blips the ways adults today fondly remember Park Place and Boardwalk.

Long live the games of old! May they prosper in the firmament forever.

"Absolutely incredible," I murmured. "Absolutely positively incredible. Do you realize how many millions of people will read this!"

Just for a moment, Laura and I stared at each other. Then we burst out laughing.

"Put your coat on," I said. "We're going out to buy the biggest bottle of champagne in Manhattan."

It was a good night. When Laura, the champagne, and I arrived at Big Walter's, he was happier than I'd ever seen him. "For my next project," he announced, "I'm going to paint a picture and hang it in the Metropolitan Museum of Art when nobody's looking."

"Big Walter, you're a genius."

"Thank you. Thank you very much. And Tom, let me say that I'm getting drunk so I might not be able to speak coherently for much longer, but it warms my heart to think that, right this minute in some place like Kansas, someone is lying in bed reading *The Mariah Project*."

"Big Walter, it makes my heart equally warm to know

that, tomorrow morning, millions of people will read 'Why I Hate Computer Video Games.' ''

When the first mega-bottle of champagne ran dry, we went out for a second. Then the orgy of mutual congratulations continued. Big Walter, in his inebriated state, informed me that I was ''a very impertant person.'' In return, I suggested that, if he ever went into politics, he'd be a star.

''Not a star,'' he corrected. ''I'd be an entire constellation; maybe even a galaxy.''

''You know something,'' Patricia observed much later, as we passed into the wee small hours of the morning. ''In some ways, you two fellows are as unalike as Genghis Khan and Judy Collins. But you really do belong together.''

Most of Saturday, I slept. Sunday I did some background reading for my new novel and took a walk in the park. Monday the mail came and, with it, the Wallace Press promotional envelope Big Walter had addressed with my name on it. Maybe now, things would begin to pick up on *The Mariah Project*. Opening the envelope, I stared down uncomprehendingly at the enclosed flier, entitled:

THE ZANY CAT
By Dorissa Gross

A cat that solves Rubik's Cube? A cat that likes guacamole enchiladas with anchovies on top? A cat that reads Sartre and Proust? Yes, sir! It's The Zany Cat!

There followed several inane paragraphs about ''the blockbuster-to-be from Wallace Press,'' closing with the exhortation, ''So rush right down to your neighborhood bookstore and buy this hilarious book!''

Picking up the phone, I dialed Wendy Schultz's number.

"Oh, yes, Mr. Hammond. It's good to hear from you. . . . Well, we had a little mix-up. . . . Yes, the wrong flier . . . That's right. All two hundred. . . . No, I understand you're upset. It's just——"

"Look, Ms. Schultz. This is my career you're fucking with. That book is my livelihood!"

"Yes, certainly. I understand. But there's no need to be upset. Everything else is running smoothly."

"Smoothly! *Smoothly!* What sort of moron are you? Orders are at thirty-one hundred. Most bookstores haven't even heard of the book. I've had a grand total of one interview. And now, after I spend God-knows-how-many hours addressing envelopes, you mail them out with a promo for the wrong book. You call that smoothly?"

"Well, Mr. Hammond. I'm afraid we're doing the best we can. We're woefully understaffed and——"

"Understaffed! A team of monkeys could do what you're doing without using their full potential."

"Mr. Hammond, really!"

"I don't want to hear any more. Look, I apologize for calling you a moron. Regardless of truth, it wasn't nice. But if——"

"Well; certainly, I agree with you about——"

"And don't interrupt me. Just hang up the phone before I say something I'll really regret."

Bordering on homicidal, I slammed down the receiver, picked it up again, and dialed Brad's number.

"Mr. Carlisle is out of town for a few days," his secretary said. "Should I ask him to call you when he returns on Monday?"

"That won't be necessary," I answered. "I guess, at this point, there's nothing much he can do anyway."

*   *   *

"I'm coping with it as best I can," I told Big Walter that night. "But it's one colossal mistake after another, and I don't understand how people can run a business like this. It borders on lack of consideration and disrespect for another person's life."

"Do you want some chopped liver? Patricia made it a few days ago; I think it's still viable."

"No, I don't want chopped liver."

"How about a beer?"

"Didn't you hear what I just said? I spent a year of my life writing a book, and the only thing anyone can find in stores are books about how to double your money and the stick-a-finger-down-your-throat bulimia diet."

"I guess people want to get rich and lose weight."

"You could train a seal to do a better job than Wallace Press is doing."

"You're exaggerating."

"Okay; maybe not a seal, but definitely a dolphin." Just for a moment, I was tempted to shout. All the pressures, all the exasperation, it was too much. But instead——

"What's the use?" I said, slumping down on the sofa. "There are forty thousand books that come out each year; maybe fifty get turned into best sellers. William Shakespeare, I'm not."

"There's still some beer left in the refrigerator," Big Walter offered, softening his voice.

"No, thanks. I'll take a rain check on it. Right now, I'm going home to bed."

The rest of the week was something of a blur. I remember some long showers, when it was easier to stay beneath the pounding water than come out and face the morning light. I spent some time with Big Walter and called Laura once or twice.

"Keep your chin up," she counseled. "If it's any consolation, things are rotten at this end, too."

"It's nice to find someone else who's candid about it," I told her. "Maybe we should get together. In grade school, they taught us that two negatives multiplied together equals a positive."

"Thanks for the offer, but some things have to be done alone. Both of us need some time to think."

By week's end, I was still down, but closer to reconciliation with my fate. The Second Great American Novel was underway and going well. Maybe it would have whatever it was *The Mariah Project* lacked.

Big Walter appeared at my doorstep on Sunday morning at 8:00.

"Have you seen *The New York Times*?" he demanded.

"What's in it—'More Opinions from a 270-Pound Jogger'?"

Thrusting the *Times Book Review Section* forward, he let out a whoop. "Take a look!"

Books in Brief: *THE MARIAH PROJECT*
by Thomas Hammond; 310 pp., Wallace Press, $14.95.

Good first novels are hard to find and good thrillers even harder. But professor-turned-author Thomas Hammond provides both with *The Mariah Project*.

CIA agent David Barrett and a young oceanologist named Carolyn Hewitt are hot on the trail of a discovery that could reshape the world. Their search takes them across the globe in a deadly game of cat-and-mouse with PLO terrorist Kaleel Rashad. The stakes? A natural hoard of energy-producing crystals somewhere in the South Pacific.

The Mariah Project is Robert Ludlum, Frederick Forsyth, and John LeCarré rolled into one—a gem of a book.

"It's a brand-new ballgame," Big Walter announced. "The sky's the limit."

21

B RAD CARLISLE WAS back from vacation and in his office Monday morning at 9:00. I arrived with a copy of the *New York Times* book review at 9:30. For a few minutes, we exchanged congratulatory words and small talk. Then came the question: "When do the ads start?"

Pushing aside some papers on his desk, Brad suppressed an uncomfortable look. "I'm not sure there'll be any." Again the look. "At present, there's no ad budget."

For a moment, we sat silent, facing each other.

"Wait a minute! For six months, all I've heard is how important the *Times* is. We can't do this because the *Times* wouldn't like it. We can't do that because the *Times* isn't ready. Well, now the *New York Times* says I've written a gem of a book. Hasn't Wallace Press ever heard of advertising?"

"Tom, it's not that we're against advertising. What I'm

trying to tell you is, there aren't enough books in stores right now to make it worthwhile.''

''I don't understand. You can't sell books because there's no advertising. You won't advertise because the stores don't have enough books. How do you plan to get *The Mariah Project* rolling?''

There was an awkward silence that lasted longer than I care to remember.

''We don't,'' Brad answered.

''What?''

''We don't. Tom, I know it's difficult, but you have to face up to reality. *The Mariah Project* is dead.''

''What!''

''It's dead, wiped out. It was stillborn, like ninety percent of everything the industry publishes.''

I wasn't sure I was hearing right.

''I went to the mat for you,'' I heard Brad saying. ''I really did. I pushed for an ad budget; I fought for you, but the purse strings belong to someone else. Maybe if we'd gotten a book-club offer, things would have been different; the manuscript might have taken off. But it didn't happen, and writers don't get paid for failure—theirs or anybody else's. It's as simple as that.''

Trying hard to maintain composure, I felt my face getting red. ''I don't understand. All year long, you've been telling me what a great book it is. Everyone loves this; everyone loves that. Now the *Times* comes through and—Jesus Christ! Cat books, diet books, double-your-money-in-four-weeks books. Don't you ever get tired of this shit?''

Eyes suddenly blazing, Brad stood up. ''Yes! It turns my stomach and, unlike you, I have to live with it every day, so cool it! Tom, I don't know where you're coming from, but I think it's time someone set you straight on the publishing business. And since you seem to be thinking in terms of sales and money, that's a good place to start. I'm thirty-two years old. I bust my ass reading manuscripts, editing books, and placating authors when things go rotten. You know what my salary is? Eighteen thousand dollars a year! That's less than a New York City transit worker makes. How do you think I feel when some imbecile who can't write a compound sentence comes in with a gimmick book and walks out with a million dollars! That's for starters. If you want more, thirty percent of the advances we pay out never earn back—including yours. Each year, a dozen writers take money without ever delivering a finished product. And, if you're interested, there's another scene I've seen played more times than I care to remember. A young writer comes in. He's gifted; he works hard; he's a wonderful guy. Then his book takes off; he makes it big, and you see this person change before your very eyes. His cheeks get fatter, his eyes grow beadier. Maybe he writes one more good novel for a lot of money, and then he starts ripping you off. His books are trash; he won't rewrite. And if he's a real prick, on top of everything else he dumps the agent who got him where he is and signs with some so-called superagent who feeds his ego. So don't feel so goddamn sorry for yourself. You wrote the book. We did our best to sell it, and that's it. Period. Wallace Press can do quite nicely without your ranting and raving and browbeating. No one made you become a writer. If you don't like the way the business operates, get out.''

Right then, we could have strangled each other, but escalating the battle didn't make sense.

"I'm sorry," Brad said as both of us backed off a bit. "People say that writers and editors have a love-hate relationship. Now you know why. It's what happens when the same person has to represent the house to the author and the author to the house.'' Pointing an index finger toward the side of his head, he pulled the trigger. "Don't get down on yourself. You wrote a good book. *The Mariah Project* might not be *Hamlet,* but it's a hell of a lot better than *Troilus and Cressida.*''

We parted on that note, friends of a sort. But the walls were beginning to tumble down, and there was something more that had to be said. On the corner of Third Avenue and 49th Street, I inserted a quarter in a pay telephone and dialed Augustus Hasson's number. As usual, the call was intercepted by Marcia Steinberg.

"I know he's busy," I told her, "but he's my agent and I'd like to see him—today."

"Tom, I'm not sure that's possible. Mr. Hasson has a full schedule."

"Then make it tonight. He can stay at the office five minutes longer."

"I'm sure it's something I can help you with."

"Look, Marcia, with all due respect, I'd like to speak with the organ grinder, not the monkey."

Whereupon I was put on hold for thirty seconds, after which Ms. Congeniality came back on the wire. "All right! Be here this afternoon at one-thirty."

That done, and with Third Avenue traffic rumbling around me, I called Laura's NBC number. "She's not in at the moment," a secretary reported.

So much for feminine consolation. Leaving Third Avenue behind, I walked home, where I was met by a return call from Laura. "I'd like to see you. In fact, I have to see you," she said.

We made plans for 3:00—a drink at the fountain café by Lincoln Center. Then, with time running out, I rehearsed what I planned to say to Augustus Hasson. A little before 1:30, without bothering to put on a jacket and tie, I arrived at the East Side town house where The Great One lived and worked. Marcia Steinberg met me at the front door and led me down the corridor. Just before the reception area, she turned left.

"Straight ahead," she said. "Mr. Hasson is waiting for you in the garden."

Following her nod, I opened an aluminum-and-glass door and walked out onto the patio. In the heart of Manhattan, a red brick path meandered to and fro. The shrubs were neatly manicured and green. Indian summer was on the wane, but sprigs of forsythia were still in bloom. Hasson was seated at a wrought-iron table with a cup of cappuccino in his hand.

"Joan Fontaine used to live there," he said, acknowledging my presence and pointing toward a town house not far from where I stood. "A great lady of the theater; I always admired her." Gesturing for me to sit, he signaled with his hand, and a maid appeared with two bowls of strawberries and a pitcher of cream. Part angry, part awed by where I was, I slipped into the chair beside him.

"Brad called," Hasson said, beginning the conversation. "I know you're angry, but don't take it out on him. If anyone's to blame for unmet expectations, the responsibility is mine." The pitcher of cream, silver, glistened in the sun. Taking a sip of cappuccino, he went on. "It's always disappointing when a book fails. No matter how much a man loves his children—and I have none—it's painfully disappointing to watch them stumble and fall. But it happens in life, and it happens with particular frequency in publishing. Most books sell less well than they would if I ran the world. That's because publishing is beset by every kind of inefficiency imaginable. At one end, there's an infinite supply of authors, with no more capital needed to go into business than paper and a typewriter. At the other extremity, publishers have an extremely poor view of the bottom line. The industry would be infinitely more efficient if there were fewer books, with more time and money put into promoting each of them. But bottom line might also mean that *The Mariah Project* would never have been published.''

Spooning a strawberry from dish to mouth, he looked off in the distance. ''My phone bill was fifteen hundred dollars this month. Did you know that?''

A stab of anger flashed through me. ''Mr. Hasson, how could I possibly know the size of your telephone bill?''

''No, I guess you couldn't.'' Still preoccupied with a faraway thought, he turned toward me. ''You know, Tom, I once wanted to be a writer. When I was thirteen, about the time most boys reach puberty and fall in love with girls, I fell in love with books. I read *Moby Dick* and *Anna Karenina* cover-to-cover, then all of Kipling, Conrad, and Mark Twain. Later, I began to write, but I could never convey a sense of excitement or put my thoughts on paper; so I decided that, rather than be a mediocre writer, I'd be the best literary agent the world had ever known. I've been successful, of course. Still, I envy your talent. When I die, the lawyers will sit down to see what I've left behind, and they'll find a pile of money—a big pile, to be sure, but still money. And when it's distributed to various philanthropic organizations, it will be no different from the money anyone else has left behind. But Tom, you're immortal. Look at what you'll leave behind. You've written a book, and no one can ever take that away from you. A hundred years from now, someone rummaging through an attic will come across *The Mariah Project* and spend an evening reading a legacy that's yours and yours alone. You're part of history.''

There really wasn't much for me to say. Maybe Augustus Hasson was being honest; maybe he was simply trying to pacify an angry client. Either way, the hurt of failure remained—but I wanted to believe him. We finished our strawberries, and The Great One stood up to walk me to the

patio door. "I love autumn," he said with genuine apprecia-
tion. "Everything seems so fresh and clean."

As we walked, he trailed behind; enough so that I slowed
so he could pull even. Whatever the reason, he seemed in
pain. "What happened?" I began to ask, wondering whether
a household accident or errant fall——

Then I realized I'd never seen Augustus Hasson walk
before.

"Polio," he said, catching my eye looking down. "When
I was seven."

> *"All fall down
> All fall down"*

I couldn't remember the rest of the rhyme. All I could
remember was a circle of children holding hands, and, at the
very end, "Ashes, ashes, all fall down." Augustus Hasson
was right about autumn, but everything around me was falling down.

I walked west toward my Lincoln Center rendezvous with
Laura. At the heart of the plaza, she was standing by the
black marble fountain, looking tired and worn. I waved, and
she came forward to hold my hand.

"Over there," she said. "By the reflecting pool, there's a
bench in the sun."

I followed her lead. The sky reminded me of the day we'd
met.

We sat on a black marble bench overlooking a sculpture by
Henry Moore.

"Tom, I'm going back to my husband. I love him in ways
I wasn't mature enough to understand."

I looked down. A gold wedding band was on the ring
finger of her left hand.

"You have to understand," Laura said, speaking softly.

"All along, I thought the problem with the marriage was Allen. But these past few months, I've reached down inside and been honest with myself. And when I did, I realized that I never gave Allen a chance. I was so busy concentrating on what was wrong that I forgot about the ways I loved him."

"Not now!" I told myself. Too many things were going wrong.

"Last night I made the decision to go home. And, when I went to Allen, I was frightened. I wasn't sure he'd take me back again. I asked if he could ever forgive me, and he answered, 'Laura, we've *both* gone through hell.' Tom, I've grown; I've changed. I'm going back for one more try."

Maybe if I argued; there was always a chance——

"Don't fight it," Laura said, responding to the look in my eyes. "You'll only make me mad, and you're the one who's entitled to be angry. I used you that day we met in the park, and maybe I've been using you all along. I've been so involved with my own problems that too often I forgot about yours. But there's one thing I haven't lost sight of, and it's desperately important to me that you understand. I care about you, Tom. For eighteen months, you've been my best friend, the only person I could talk with about everything; the most important person in my world and also the best one. As long as I live, I'll never forget the days and nights we spent together. They were some of the happiest moments I've had. Time after time, I compared you to Allen, and you came out ahead on every score except one—I love him. I really do. I've been fighting you all along, and finally I realized that it was because I wasn't willing to give up Allen. My emotional ties to him are stronger than my ties to you. And Tom, this is very difficult for me to say, but I don't love you. We're too different from one another, and we have very different ideas of love. You're looking for something that doesn't exist in me. Maybe you'll find it; I hope so. But whatever happens,

I'll always be grateful to you. You'll always have a piece of my heart.''

I couldn't talk. My throat was clogged, and my cheeks were beginning to puff up below my eyes.

"Don't worry," Laura said with a smile. "You're wonderful. You'll go on to be rich and famous and get married and have children and live happily ever after. You're so goddamn efficient, it couldn't happen any other way."

"And if I louse it up?"

"You won't." Again the smile, belied by tears that glistened. "I guess the nature of things is we won't be seeing each other anymore. But I'll miss you terribly. You've touched me; you and Big Walter, both of you. And not too many people have done that in my life."

"Do I get a kiss good-bye?"

Gently, she ran her hand across my cheek. "Good-bye, Tom. And don't worry. Someday you'll find what you're looking for."

Big Walter was in the boiler room, his face streaked with grime and sweat, when I arrived. One look spoke volumes. "You look cheerful," he said. Then, laying aside his wrench and pliers, he listened as I poured out my heart: the stillborn novel, Laura, everything else that was wrong with my life. It wasn't a happy story.

"Could you do me a favor?" he asked when I was done.

"What is it?"

"Stop feeling so sorry for yourself. It's making me sick."

All I could do was stare.

"Tom, if I thought it would do any good, I'd go upstairs and bring down Patricia to give you a hug. In fact, I'm half-inclined to do it myself. But I think it's time this orgy of self-pity came to an end." Sitting on an overturned crate, Big Walter gestured for me to do likewise. "I know you're feeling vulnerable and kicked around, and, believe me, I'm sorry. But if you have to feel sorry for someone, feel sorry for Laura and Allen. Think about what they went through this past year and what the two of them will have to go through together to patch up their marriage. You're no worse off than you were a year ago; probably even a little better. You had a good time while it lasted, and you're wiser for it all.''

"And what about *The Mariah Project*—a year of my life gone forever.''

"That,'' Big Walter said softly, "is where you make me sick. You got screwed—I know that. A bunch of well-meaning people loused up your book and it hurts; it has to hurt. But look at yourself! You sat down, wrote a novel, and had it published. It got great reviews and, for all you know, there could be a movie deal tomorrow. You happen to have the best agent in the business, and you're part-way into a second novel. You've shown you can earn a living as a writer, and I'd give my right arm for that.''

Reaching out with his voice, Big Walter went on. "Tom, I don't think you understand; I don't think you have any idea what it's like to get up in the morning, to go to the mailbox and hope there's *nothing* there—because if someone wants a screenplay, they telephone, and all that ever comes by mail are rejections. Do you know what it's like to be married to the most wonderful woman in the world, and want to have children—and be forced to wait because one of us isn't making any money and the other has to keep working a little longer? And do you know what it's like to live in a world where dollars are the measure of success, to know you're just as smart and just as good as anyone else, but somehow the rest of the world doesn't see it that way? Anytime you want to trade, you can have my job as building superintendent and I'll take your gift for novels—but, if we do trade, I keep Patricia.''

There was a long pause while I absorbed what was happening.

"Hey, Big Walter."

"What is it?"

"Thanks."

Reaching out, he stretched an arm around my shoulders. "Think nothing of it. That's what friends are for. Now, if you'll excuse me, I have work to do. One of the tenants is screaming bloody murder because there isn't enough hot water."

"Which one?"

"Patricia."

I went for a walk. The boiler room was too dreary to stay any longer, and there wasn't much else to do. I figured the park might take my mind off my problems.

For a while, it worked. The sky was blue, and it was quite nice walking along the promenade overlooking the river. I even decided that Big Walter and I should collaborate on a screen version of *The Mariah Project* with Paul Newman in the lead. For sure, we'd make a million dollars.

Then Laura filtered back into my thoughts. Part of me wanted to go back and fight for her, but I knew it was futile. From the very start, something inside had told me she'd go back to Allen. Too often, she and I were just going through the motions. There were moments when we were making love, when suddenly something would move across her eyes like a shadow, and I'd known she was thinking of him. In my mind, I'd denied it, but inside I had known. The signs were there. I'd simply chosen to ignore them.

The October sun dipped toward the horizon on its downward flight. The air grew colder—a chill reminder that, in two months, autumn would be gone.

"Cheer up," I told myself. "Don't get down; there's no point to it. Life goes on."

Besides, on reflection, it seemed that maybe Big Walter was right. Maybe life wasn't so bad after all; maybe fate was kind and things would work out in the end—especially since ten yards ahead, leaning against the wall looking down at the Hudson River, was an absolutely stunning vision: the unmistakable form of The Fantasy Jogger.

Trembling, I walked toward her.

She turned . . . and there was eye contact, followed by a warm, welcoming smile.

"Hi!" I ventured.

"I remember you," The Fantasy Jogger said.

Afterward

THE FUNNY THING is, she was pretty much the way I'd imagined her. Warm, gentle, sexy, smart. Twenty-eight years old; married at twenty-two, divorced two years later. Her first book had come out during the summer and been triaged by one of New York's better publishers. Now she was working on another. We walked along the path where I'd first seen her, through the park, onto Riverside Drive. And then something happened which made me realize that the gods were merciful and on my side.

"It's strange," she said as our hands brushed together. "In a lot of ways, you remind me of the hero in my novel."